D0194990

IN THE FOOTSTEPS OF CRAZY HORSE

BY

Joseph Marshall III

ILLUSTRATIONS BY

Jim Yellowhawk

AMULET BOOKS NEW YORK

Library of Congress Cataloging-in-Publication Data

Marshall, Joseph, 1945–
In the footsteps of Crazy Horse / Joseph Marshall ; illustrated by Jim Yellowhawk.
pages cm
Includes bibliographical references.
ISBN 978-1-4197-0785-8 (hardback)
[1. Self-confidence—Fiction. 2. Crazy Horse, approximately 1842–1877—Fiction.
3. Lakota Indians—Fiction. 4. Indians of North America—Great Plains—Fiction.
5. Grandfathers—Fiction. 6. Great Plains—Fiction. 7. Great Plains—History—
19th century—Fiction.] I. Yellowhawk, Jim, 1958– illustrator. II. Title.
PZ.1.M35543In 2015
[Fic]—dc23
2015002042

Printed and bound in U.S.A.
10 9 8 7 6 5 4 3 2 1

ABRAMS
THE ART OF BOOKS SINCE 1949

115 West 18th Street
New York, NY 10011
www.abramsbooks.com

IN LOVING MEMORY OF

Connie West Marshall

1949–2013

—J.M. III

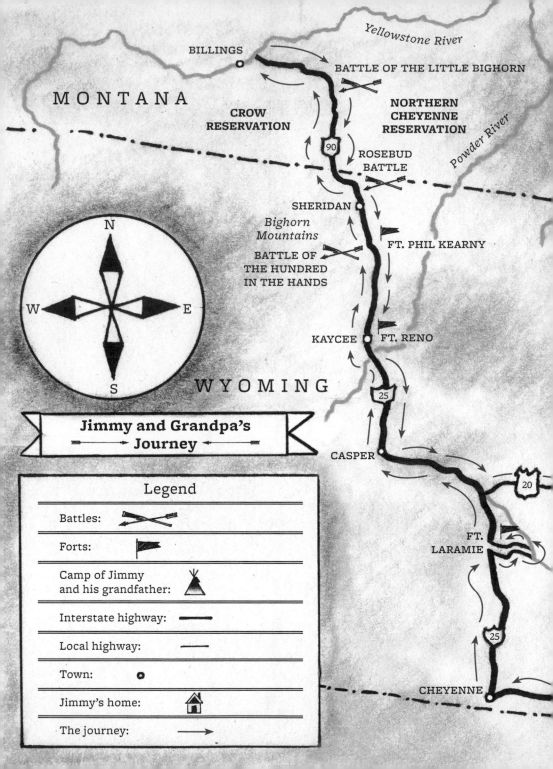

1

Rosebud Sioux Indian Reservation

JIMMY McCLEAN WALKED AMONG THE BUFFALO BERRY thickets along the Smoking Earth River. It was a warm afternoon in late May. School was done for the week, and almost for the year. Jimmy was glad of that. He was tired of being teased for having blue eyes.

The river cut through the valley below the town of Cold River. Cold River was on the northern edge of the Rosebud

Sioux Indian Reservation in South Dakota. Jimmy lived with his parents in a modular house on the east side. That was okay. But it was not okay that he lived two blocks from Cold River Public School. He hated school. Corky Brin and Jesse Little Horse were two of the reasons. Maybe they were the only reasons. No, he didn't like math, or PE, either. In PE he had to hold hands with a girl. It was a game everyone had to play. But holding hands with a girl—that was embarrassing.

Corky teased him about it, and so did Jesse. Corky was white, and Jesse was Lakota. They didn't like each other, but they seemed to bond over teasing Jimmy.

Jimmy had blue eyes and light-brown hair. Other Lakota children had black hair, brown skin, and brown eyes. They had family names like Little Horse, Turning Bear, Bissonette, or Black Wolf. This was another reason for Corky and Jesse to tease him.

McClean was a white name. It was his other grandfather's name, a man he had never met. Angus McClean was his dad's dad. His mom was Anne, and her last name was High Eagle. But now she was Anne McClean. Jimmy's dad was James McLean Sr. No one called him Jimmy. James Sr. was half Lakota and half white. His hair was dark brown and his skin was a bit lighter than most Lakota people's, but his eyes were brown. Jimmy was James McClean Jr.

His dad's mom was Madeline Bear, from the Pine Ridge Reservation, in the western part of the state. It all meant—as his mom explained—that three parts of Jimmy were Lakota and one part was white. That part was Scottish, to be exact.

"The problem is," Anne McClean would say, "your three Lakota parts are all hidden inside. Your one white part is on the outside."

Jimmy understood what she meant, but it didn't make him feel any better. It was the main reason Corky and Jesse teased him.

"You're just an Indian pretending to be white" was what Corky liked to say.

"Who ever heard of a Lakota with blue eyes and a name like McClean?" Jesse would say.

Jimmy's usual reply always infuriated Jesse even more. *"Malakota yelo!"* he would yell. Which meant "I am Lakota" in Lakota. Jesse did not understand or speak Lakota.

According to Jesse, a blue-eyed Lakota was strange. And one who spoke Lakota was even stranger.

Jimmy never fought, because he was eleven and Jesse was twelve and bigger. Corky was bigger than Jesse, so every argument with either of them was a loss, because it made Jimmy feel small and weak.

Now he found refuge, again, in the trees and thickets by the Smoking Earth River. Here the trees accepted him just the way he was, blue eyes and all. So did the grasses, and the birds, and the rabbits. Here, by the river, he was just a boy.

On Saturday morning Jimmy awoke to the sound of his grandfather Nyles's voice. He hurried to the bathroom to splash water on his face. In the kitchen he found his parents and Grandpa Nyles having coffee and talking in English. Sometimes they spoke in Lakota, but not this morning.

"Hey, sleepyhead," James called out to his son. "I thought you were going to snore all morning." James was in his dark-blue uniform. He was a tribal police officer and sometimes worked on Saturdays. Today was one of those sometimes.

Jimmy let his dad rumple his hair. "Hey, Grandpa," he said as he hugged his mom. She was a Head Start teacher and did not work on Saturdays. "What's the haps?"

Nyles High Eagle's brown face had deep creases. He was tall, and his hair was long and black, sprinkled with gray. He always wore it in a single braid. A wide smile beamed for his grandson. "Got some chores," he said in a strong, soft voice. "Means riding horses, though. I know you don't like to do that."

"Who told you that?" Jimmy teased back. "I was born riding horses." It was his favorite thing to do. Well, next to being with his grandpa.

"A meadowlark," answered Grandpa Nyles. "Just yesterday one told me that. Mom and Dad say as soon as you have breakfast and get ready, we can go."

"I'm not hungry," Jimmy said. "I'll be ready in a sec."

"There'll be breakfast waiting for you," Anne McClean said. "Take a shower, get dressed, and take some clothes for overnight. You're not leaving this house without breakfast."

Jimmy nodded and hurried away to his room. There was

no arguing with his mom when she used that tone of voice. Anyway, he was spending the night with Grandpa Nyles and Grandma Sarah! They lived ten miles out of town, on a small horse ranch.

Jimmy smiled ear to ear as he loped across the prairie with Grandpa Nyles. He was riding Little Warrior, a small but sturdy buckskin quarter horse. Grandpa was on Dancer, a muscular bay quarter horse stallion. Grandpa Nyles had a small herd of horses. There was the stallion, three mares, their colts, and two geldings for riding. Little Warrior was a gelding.

Their chore was checking Grandpa Nyles's twelve miles of fences. Jimmy knew Grandpa Nyles hated barbed wire, but it did keep the neighbors' cattle out of the horse pastures. So it was important to check the fences regularly, just in case there were breaks or any loose wire.

They stopped along Horse Creek, which flowed into the Smoking Earth River. Grandpa wanted to rest the horses and let them graze. Besides, it was always good to relax in the shade of some big, tall cottonwood trees. Jimmy took a long stick and poked around in the grasses before he sat down. It was a way to scare away snakes. Grandpa had taught him that.

Sitting against the trunk of a giant cottonwood tree, they listened to the creek gurgling and watched the horses munch on grass. This was the sort of thing Jimmy wanted to do the rest of his life.

"So them boys been teasing you again?" Grandpa asked suddenly.

Jimmy nodded. "Yeah," he said softly.

"Well," drawled Grandpa Nyles, a blade of grass between his teeth, "what's their main problem?"

"I don't know." Jimmy shrugged. "They say I'm not Lakota."

"Why? Because your skin is light and you have blue eyes?"

Jimmy shrugged again. "I guess so."

"I think I can settle this whole issue once and for all," declared Grandpa Nyles.

Jimmy perked up. "You going to beat them up?" He could almost see that.

"No," Grandpa replied with a chuckle. "Don't think we can change them boys. But we might change how you look at things."

"What do you mean, Grandpa?"

"Well, the answer to that question is a long one. It means you and me are going on a trip, soon as school is out. Are you up for that?"

Jimmy sat up straight. This was too good to be true. "You mean, like camping?"

"Yeah, there'll be some camping. A lot of driving. And seeing some interesting and important places."

Jimmy could not believe his ears. He couldn't wait!

"One more thing," added Grandpa. "You remember the stories about Crazy Horse, don't you?"

"Yeah. You told me he was the greatest Lakota warrior, a long time ago."

"Did I tell you what he looked like?"

Jimmy shook his head. "No, I don't think so."

"Well," said his grandpa, "let me show you what he looked like. Let's go to the creek."

Puzzled, Jimmy followed his grandpa.

"Now," said Grandpa Nyles, kneeling carefully at the edge of the bank. "Look into the water."

Jimmy looked down, but all he could see was their reflections.

Grandpa pointed at Jimmy's. "Who do you see there?" he asked.

"Me—that's me, Grandpa."

"Are you sure? I could swear that's Crazy Horse when he was your age. Though his hair was probably a bit longer."

Jimmy was still puzzled, but now he was curious, too. "For reals?"

"Yeah. My great-grandfather—your great-great-grand-father—was born in 1860. He saw Crazy Horse, as close as you are to me. He said Crazy Horse had light skin, like you, and brown hair, like you. He didn't have blue eyes. But some boys teased him, too."

Jimmy stared at his own reflection in the water. *No way,* he thought. *I don't look like Crazy Horse.*

"Yeah," sighed Grandpa, as if he had read Jimmy's

thoughts. "I could swear that's young Crazy Horse looking at me. Of course, when he was a boy, they called him Light Hair."

Jimmy couldn't take his eyes off his own face looking back at him.

"Tell you what," Grandpa Nyles continued. "Now that you have some idea what he looked like, want to go see where he lived, and played, and hunted—all that stuff?"

Jimmy looked at his grandpa and smiled.

2

Bear Butte

JIMMY HAD BEEN TO RAPID CITY MANY TIMES. SOME-
times he went with his grandparents and sometimes with
his parents. Now and then they all went together. Rapid
City was a large town on the northeast edge of the Black
Hills. The Black Hills were in the western part of the state.
They weren't just hills—they were the only mountains in
South Dakota. Actually, they were the only mountains on the
Great Plains.

Today, a week after summer vacation had started, he and Grandpa were on the top of Bear Butte. It stood northwest of Rapid City, near the town of Sturgis. The air was cool. They had climbed the winding Summit Trail to reach the top. It was called Bear Butte because from the south it looked like a bear lying on its stomach. It was sacred to the Lakota. It was a special place to pray.

The view was spectacular. To the west were the Black Hills, and to the east were the endless prairies. Jimmy and his grandpa stepped onto the wooden platform at the top. Grandpa Nyles took pictures and then offered pipe tobacco to the four directions.

He pointed southwest, toward the dark line of mountains. "Rapid Creek starts in the hills, flows east, and goes through Rapid City. Then it joins the Cheyenne River farther to the east."

Jimmy nodded. He could not really see the creek, but he followed where his grandpa was pointing. He knew Rapid Creek had something to do with Crazy Horse.

"Crazy Horse was born somewhere along that creek," the old man said. "Somewhere in sight of Bear Butte, according to most stories. So I thought this would be a good place to start our journey."

"You think Crazy Horse stood up here?" Jimmy asked.

"I'm sure he did," Grandpa Nyles replied.

They stayed for a while, taking in the scenery and the fresh air.

"Well," said Grandpa at last. "How about we start back down? We've got a long way to go on this journey."

They drove south from Rapid City and after two hours crossed the South Dakota–Nebraska border. Jimmy had driven to Nebraska before with his dad. They had gone to a town called North Platte, to look at a pickup truck. But traveling with Grandpa Nyles was different. Grandpa told stories about things they saw, like coyotes, crows, a white-tailed deer, and hawks. In a way, it was like watching TV, because he was such a good storyteller.

"A long time ago," Grandpa said as he and Jimmy rode down the highway, "people and animals could understand each other's languages. A person could understand what a hawk said. The hawk could understand people. But things changed. Animals and people don't understand each other anymore. That's sad."

"What changed, Grandpa?"

"Oh, people began to think they were better than anything. Better than animals."

Not long after they crossed the state line, they came to a town called Chadron. From there they continued south. It was a long drive, and eventually they came to a sign that read ASH HOLLOW STATE HISTORICAL PARK. From there they drove north a ways.

"I have a friend here," Grandpa Nyles told Jimmy. "He's a rancher, and he gave permission for us to camp on his land."

Jimmy waved his hand. "Why is it so hilly, Grandpa?" he asked.

"These are the Sandhills. They go a long way to the east," his grandfather said.

They drove across a cattle guard gate in the woven wire fence. For a few miles they followed a worn pasture trail. As Jimmy's curiosity grew, they came to a meadow that was hidden among the low, grassy hills. There were no roads or houses anywhere. Jimmy liked the feeling of being away from everything. Just like the old, old days his grandpa talked about. No houses, no fences, no power poles. It was cool.

"Our first camp," Grandpa Nyles announced. Jimmy eagerly jumped out of the truck.

They had the dome pop-up tent up in no time, and soon Grandpa had a small fire going in the fire pit he had dug. He already had prepared two big slabs of skillet bread—just flour mixed with water. When the skillet was hot, he cooked them. They looked like two big dark pancakes. Soup was heating in a saucepan on a metal grate over the fire. Jimmy was wearing his face-splitting grin again. This was the good life. He even pretended the old pickup was a horse.

"Crazy Horse was here," Grandpa Nyles declared suddenly. "Somewhere in this very area, around 1855. He was twelve or thirteen then, and still called Light Hair."

"Did he live here?"

"No, but other Lakota people did. Our Sicangu ancestors came this far south. Light Hair's birth mother died when he was about four. Later, his father, Crazy Horse, remarried. He had two new wives. They were sisters and Sicangu Lakota. The Sicangu people hunted in this area."

"How could Light Hair's dad have two wives at the same time?"

"Some men did in those days. So the two new wives went to live with their new husband and his children, Light Hair and his older sister. That was in what is now eastern Wyoming."

Jimmy was confused. "So if Light Hair didn't live here, then why are we here?"

"He was here visiting relatives," Grandpa Nyles said, taking the soup off the grate.

"Was it something brave?"

"For sure. He rescued a young woman near here, so she would be safe."

"Rescued her from what?"

Grandpa Nyles looked at the low hills around them, covered with tall grass. A slow, lazy wind was making them wave. Like they were dancing together. A look came into Grandpa's eyes. Jimmy could not tell where he was looking.

But he was definitely seeing something. It was his story-telling face.

"Well, let me tell you the way it was, why Light Hair rescued that young woman. . . ."

The way it was—1855

Light Hair and several other Lakota boys galloped their horses over hill after hill. It was exciting to feel the wind against their faces. It was a warm early-autumn day in the Moon of Leaves Turning Color. "Moon" was the Lakota word for month. The Lakota did not number the years. For other people it was 1855.

They were in what is now western Nebraska. Hunting had been their task for the day. They were going back to the village, having shot one antelope and one deer with their bows and arrows. That would feed several families. At the top of a hill they stopped. They did not want to exhaust their horses.

Light Hair patted his horse's neck. He was slender, with

two long braids that were dark brown, not black like coal, like the hair of the other Lakota boys. His skin was not deep brown, either, like his companions'. He was not pale, just noticeably less brown, though everyone was a shade browner from being constantly in the sun.

He looked east toward where the village was. Little Thunder was the headman there. Light Hair was here on a visit with his two Sicangu mothers' relatives. It had been a good summer. When autumn was over, he would go back to his own village. That was to the west, north of the Shell River and east of the Medicine Bow Mountains.

Something caught his eye. At first it looked like a flock of birds. Then Light Hair realized it was smoke, blowing in the breeze. It was near the village. He pointed, and everyone saw the long, dark wisps.

"It's a grass fire!" White Bear said. He was fourteen and tall for his age. "Come on! We have to warn everyone!"

The riders took off at a gallop. Up one slope and down another, they raced for the village. Light Hair and his fast bay horse pulled far ahead. Grass fires were dangerous, especially in the autumn. Grass and shrubs were dry and burned fast.

Just west of the village he pulled back on the single rein to stop his horse. From a low hill he saw the village. It was a sight he would never forget.

The village itself was burning! Lodges, lodgepoles, and meat racks—everything seemed to be on fire. Several horses were running away from the billowing smoke and yellow-orange flames. For a moment, Light Hair did not know what to do. Then he leaned forward and kicked his horse into yet another gallop. Exhausted or not, the horse responded willingly. Light Hair was glad. There was trouble ahead, and perhaps people were hurt.

At the distance of a long bowshot from the village, the scene was terrifying. The ground was scorched black where the flames had passed. Every buffalo-hide lodge was burning or had already been turned into a pile of ashes. Horses and dogs were running about in fright and confusion.

As he approached the village, Light Hair saw bundles on the ground. His companions caught up to him. They all stopped and stared. It was all they could do. None of them had ever seen a village burning. They were shocked into not moving.

"The wind isn't strong enough to move a fire that fast through the entire village," someone said.

"What shall we do?" asked one of the boys.

"Help anyone we can find!" shouted Light Hair, and he kicked his horse into a gallop once again. The other boys hesitated a moment before they followed him.

Light Hair and his bay horse soon reached the edge of the village. The horse was afraid of the flames. Or perhaps it was the stench of burned and burning things. It was then that Light Hair saw that the bundles on the ground were people. He was sick to his stomach. At the sight of a burning pile of clothing, the horse jumped sideways. Light Hair was caught by surprise and fell off. Clinging to the rein, he jumped to his feet. The smoke and stench were too much for the horse. He pulled away from Light Hair and galloped off.

White Bear arrived, a frightened, horrified look on his face. "There are people on the ground, not moving!" he called out.

Yellow Eyes joined them, his horse skittish as well. "I saw people walking," he said, pointing to the north. "Some women, and men on horses, on that hill."

Looking through the swirling haze of smoke, they all saw dark shapes in the distance.

"Long Knives!" hissed White Bear. "Long Knives with guns!"

The boys looked at one another. Fear and confusion were on all their faces. The Long Knives were the soldiers of the white people. Last year they had attacked a Sicangu village near Fort Laramie. Long Knives everywhere were known to shoot at any Lakota, alone or in a village. Here they had probably started the fire.

"Go see," said Light Hair. "If they are Long Knives, see what is happening. Don't let them spot you! I'll see if there are any of our people still here."

White Bear and the other boys rode hesitantly down into the valley. There they could stay out of sight. Light Hair watched them forlornly for a moment. Long Knives were known to attack any Lakota—man, woman, or child. They were mean people—if they were people at all.

Light Hair reluctantly looked around at the burned village. The only people he saw were on the ground. None of them were moving. He went from one to another, a sick feeling in his stomach. Some of the bodies were small children. All the while, acrid smoke swirled around him. Suddenly he heard a faint cry. He stopped and listened, and it came again. He followed the faint whimper, and it led him down the long slope. Finally he came to a bank. Beneath an overhang he saw someone under a covering of grass and twigs. It was a young woman. He recognized her. She was a Cheyenne woman who was married to a Lakota man. She was weeping softly.

Her name was Yellow Woman. Light Hair touched her on the shoulder. She looked at him with a tear-streaked face.

"I know you," she whispered to Light Hair.

"What happened?" he asked softly.

"Long Knives came," she sobbed. "They shot people. My husband is . . . He's gone." She wept again. "So is my baby." She pointed to a small mound of dirt under the bank.

Light Hair helped Yellow Woman finish covering her baby.

She sat staring at the small mound. "I hid in a cave along the river with some others. We waited until the Long Knives left and then came out. Some of our people fled that way," she said, pointing northeast. "Maybe they got away—I don't know. I stayed to find my husband and bury my baby."

Soft hoofbeats startled them.

It was White Bear. "Long Knives are taking women and children north," he told them somberly. "We will follow them."

Light Hair nodded and pointed at Yellow Woman. "I will help her," he said.

"Good," replied White Bear. "Then we will see you later. Watch out. There may be more Long Knives."

"You, too," warned Light Hair.

Then White Bear was gone. It did not take long for the sound of hoofbeats to fade away.

"What shall we do?" Yellow Woman asked, her voice like that of a small girl.

"Maybe we should follow those people who went northeast," he suggested. "We can find their trail."

After catching his horse, Light Hair tied drag poles to the bay. On the frame he put Yellow Woman, who was again sobbing softly. Leading the horse and keeping a sharp eye out, he took them northeast. It was not hard to find foot- and hoofprints in the grass and soil, as well as the imprints of many drag poles.

Light Hair looked back at the burned-down village. He wanted to cry because there was nothing he could do for those who were left behind. There were many bodies scattered over the scorched ground.

At sundown Light Hair made a cold camp with no fire to show their presence in the dark. He shared what little food he had with Yellow Woman. At dawn they began traveling again and did not stop until they came to a small creek, where they drank and watered the horse.

They kept traveling through the day. Soon they came into a very hilly area of the prairies, with tall grass and sandy soil. Yellow Woman had stopped weeping, but she was silent most of the time. Light Hair managed to shoot a rabbit with his bow and arrow. He risked a fire to cook it and was glad. The fresh food strengthened them both. They continued on, and at sundown he smelled smoke from a distant fire. The next day they were spotted by lookouts from a camp hidden among the sandy hills.

It was a sad and somber camp. Most of the people were glad to see Light Hair and Yellow Woman. Some didn't react at all. There were wounded and injured people among those who had fled. Light Hair was glad to find Spotted Tail, his uncle, among them. He was the overall Sicangu leader. One of the men told Light Hair how fiercely Spotted Tail had fought. He had knocked down at least ten Long Knives before he was shot and seriously wounded. But he would get well. Spotted Tail was a strong and tall man, a powerful warrior. Light Hair's mothers were Spotted Tail's sisters.

Light Hair stayed in the camp for two days. When Yellow Woman no longer cried herself to sleep, he decided to leave. He wanted to go home, to his own family. He was sure they would have heard of the attack by now. Light Hair wanted his father and mothers to know he was not hurt. He was told the camp would move farther east in two days. Two more days would give the wounded time to rest and heal.

Yellow Woman did not want him to leave, yet she understood that he must.

"I will never forget you and what you did for me," she said with tears in her eyes.

"Light Hair was only a few years older than you when this happened," Grandpa Nyles said to Jimmy.

"So did he go home?" Jimmy wanted to know. "And what happened to the women and children who had been taken captive?"

"He did go home, and he told his family what had happened," Grandpa Nyles said. "It wasn't the last time he stayed with his mothers' relatives, though. As for the captives, well, the Long Knives kept them for a while, then let them go."

Jimmy was sad and angry. "Why did they attack our people?"

"To punish them for something they didn't do," said Grandpa Nyles.

"What?" Jimmy was confused.

"That is another story about Light Hair," promised the old man. "That will come later in our journey. Now it's time to put out the fire and turn in."

The next morning Jimmy and his grandpa drove south and got on Interstate 80 going west. After a few hours they crossed into Wyoming and arrived in Cheyenne. They stopped for a bite to eat and to put gas in the truck, and then they went north on Interstate 25. At the exit for a town called Guernsey, they turned east.

3

The Oregon Trail

IT WAS WINDY AND CLOUDY. THEY DROVE THROUGH THE small town of Guernsey, and late in the afternoon they stopped along the highway. Crossing the fence, Jimmy followed his grandpa to the top of a hill. They sat down among some bristly green soap plants. Grandpa Nyles pointed at the river in the valley below them. "That is called the North Platte River," he said. "Our people called it the Shell River.

Now, if you look carefully, you can see some deep ruts just this side of the river."

"Yeah," said Jimmy. "I see them. Looks like some big trucks got stuck in the mud."

Grandpa Nyles chuckled. "Well, guess what? Those ruts, those tracks, are over a hundred and fifty years old."

Jimmy was astonished. "For reals?"

"For reals."

"Wow! Who made them?"

"Wagons. Thousands of them."

Jimmy let out a whistle. "Thousands?"

"Ever heard of the Oregon Trail?"

"Yeah, we studied it in school."

"Before it was called the Oregon Trail," Grandpa Nyles explained, "it was known by the Lakota and other tribes as the Shell River Road. And before that, it was a trail used by animals, like buffalo. It's an old, old trail."

He paused for a moment. "So do you know why we're here?"

"Crazy Horse was here?"

"You got it. He was still Light Hair when he first saw wagons on this trail. Hundreds . . . thousands of them."

Jimmy stared at the deep ruts. He knew about trails. Lots of animals or people or cars traveling made trails. They wore out the grass and made marks on the ground. *How many wagons made those deep marks?* he wondered. He could not imagine what hundreds and thousands of wagons looked like.

"Imagine," said Grandpa Nyles, "if one day you suddenly saw hundreds of flying saucers in the sky. What would you think? How would you feel?"

"I'd be scared," admitted Jimmy. "And . . . and I'd wonder who was in them. The flying saucers, I mean."

Grandpa Nyles smiled. "You know, I'd bet that's exactly what Light Hair thought, back in about, oh, 1852."

The way it was—summer 1852

A slow, lazy breeze floated through the grasses. It was a hot summer afternoon. From the top of a hill, young Light Hair looked to the west. The front of the line of covered wagons went out of sight over a far hill. He looked to the east. Wagons at the back of the line were just coming over the horizon.

A few riders were on either side of the wagons. Some people walked, but no one seemed to be in a hurry.

Light Hair was careful to stay down behind the grasses. Beside him was Little Hawk, his uncle, who was just as astonished at the sight of the endless line of wagons. One after another, pulled by oxen. Since warriors always carried their weapons, Uncle Little Hawk had his black powder percussion rifle with him. His bow and arrows were tied on his horse.

"Are they people?" Light Hair whispered.

"I think so," Uncle Little Hawk replied. "But not like us. Their skin is pale, and many of the men have beards. Their clothing is different."

"Where are they going?" the boy wondered.

"Somewhere to the west. They have been doing this for four or five summers now. But I don't remember seeing this many."

Light Hair and his uncle watched in silence. They had seen wagons before. The Long Knives at Fort Laramie used them. Wagons hauled soldiers and other people. They also *carried food, flat wood, guns and powder, tools, clothing, and even water. All the things the white people needed and used. But never had the Lakota seen so many at once. Wagons were end to end, from one horizon to the other. And even more people with them.*

Light Hair did not know what to think. In a way, he was scared, and he wondered if his uncle was or if his father, Crazy Horse, was.

"As long as they keep going," Little Hawk said, "that will be good. We don't want those people staying here, on our lands. They leave their trash behind and scare away the buffalo. The wagon wheels leave marks—they scar the land."

Jimmy looked at the empty land along the river. Some cattle grazed on the other side. A few antelope could be seen.

"How many wagons went through here?" he asked his grandpa.

"Hard to know, but history says that three hundred and fifty thousand people traveled on the Oregon Trail."

Jimmy was astonished. "Three hundred and fifty thousand? Wow! That's . . . that's a lot of counting."

"For sure. They started from the state of Missouri, went by here, and ended up in California or Oregon. They did that for twenty years."

"That's older than me," Jimmy declared. "What happened to them all?"

"Well, that's the problem," Grandpa Nyles said with a sigh. "Some of them decided to stay. Later, more came to stay. They farmed and raised cattle and sheep. They forced our people off their own lands."

"Did our people try to stop them?"

"Yes, they did. There were battles. When Light Hair became Crazy Horse, he fought in many of them."

Fort Laramie

Fort Laramie National Historic Site was a group of old buildings. They stood around a yard that seemed very large to Jimmy. People were walking around and looking into the buildings.

Grandpa Nyles drove into the parking lot and stopped. "Remember the ruts back there, along the river?"

"Yeah," Jimmy replied.

"Well, that trail came to this place, and then went on far-ther to the west. This place is Fort Laramie. It's been here a long time."

Jimmy looked around. There was a wagon beside one of the buildings. Near another wagon stood a group of men in blue uniforms.

"Are those Long Knives?" Jimmy wanted to know.

"In a way," Grandpa Nyles answered. "They are reenact-ors. They come here and play the part of soldiers. They talk to the tourists."

"Where are the Indians?" Jimmy asked.

"Good question. Come on, let's look around."

"Okay. So Crazy Horse was here?"

"Yeah, he sure was. He was here, as Light Hair and as Crazy Horse."

The way it was—September 1851

Light Hair could not believe the number of people. He could stand in one place, turn in a circle, and there were people, lodges, and horses everywhere he looked. All were camped along Horse Creek, a day's ride east of Fort Laramie, the Long Knives' outpost.

"Where did they come from?" he asked They Are Afraid of Her, one of his mothers.

"All over," she replied as she sliced wild turnips into an iron kettle. "From the south, west, north, and east."

"Why are we here?" he asked.

"Because the white peace talkers invited all of them and us to come," she replied.

"I heard some people talking, but I couldn't understand them," Light Hair told her.

"Yes. Many different people means different languages," she said. "There are our friends the Arapaho and the Cheyenne. Our enemies, too, the Crow. Then the Assiniboine, Mandan, Hidatsa, and Arikara. Our relatives the Dakota and the Nakota are here, too."

"Why?"

They Are Afraid of Her chuckled. "Because of the white people in the wagons on the Shell River Road. They're afraid we might attack them. So the peace talkers want us to promise to leave them alone."

"*Then maybe they should just stay away,*" said Light Hair.

His mother laughed. "*That's what most of the people here think. Now, go find your brother and the two of you stay close to our lodge. I don't want you wandering away. It's easy to get lost.*"

Light Hair found his little brother, Whirlwind. He was called that because he was always on the move, first going in one direction, then another. "*Come here,*" he said to the younger boy. "*Mother wants us to stay close.*"

"*Let's go look at those horses!*" begged Whirlwind. "*See, over there? They have little black spots all over them.*"

"*All right—but just for a little while,*" Light Hair said, giving in.

They hurried through the groups of people while avoiding the barking dogs. Light Hair took his little brother by the hand. He had never seen so many people in one place. Men stood in groups together talking. Older boys rode by on horses. Women called out for their children. Others tended to kettles hanging over cooking fires. Smaller children *played by the lodges. And everywhere he looked, it seemed there were more horses than people.*

He suddenly felt very small.

"That was the Council on Horse Creek," said Grandpa Nyles. "East of here. History calls it the Fort Laramie Treaty Council of 1851. The people came because they were curious about what the white peace talkers wanted. They were told all the Indians were not to bother the people in the wagons on the Oregon Trail. Also because the whites offered gifts. Being asked not to bother those people seemed kind of silly, because it was the wagon people who always started the trouble. Some of them would shoot at Indians. The tribes signed the treaty. But after Light Hair became Crazy Horse, he was here again. Other than that, he stayed away. He didn't like this place."

"Well, why did he come back?" Jimmy wondered.

"Horses," replied Grandpa Nyles. "He led a raid. Crazy Horse and several other Lakota warriors swept through here like a sudden wind. They took the Long Knives' horses. The Long Knives chased them, but they couldn't catch them."

Grandpa Nyles turned and pointed west, beyond a two-story building. "They came from that direction." Then he pointed toward the other side of the large open space. "Most of the Long Knives' horses were picketed there. Pawnee scout horses, too."

"Pawnee?" Jimmy asked.

"The Long Knives used them a lot as scouts, against other Indians."

"Did they take *all* the horses from here?"

"No, I don't think so. A lot of them, though."

Jimmy looked around, imagining Lakota warriors on horseback. He could see them racing across the open area. He could hear the drumlike pounding of hooves.

"Why did they do that?" he asked his grandfather.

Grandpa Nyles smiled. "Well, because they could. And because Crazy Horse wanted to annoy the Long Knives."

Jimmy smiled broadly. "I think he did that."

Grandpa Nyles was smiling as well. "Yeah, he did, for sure. But there was an incident that happened near here, when he was still Light Hair—something that caused the Long Knives to attack Little Thunder's village."

"You mean when Light Hair helped Yellow Woman? What happened?"

Grandpa Nyles took on his storytelling face again. "Yeah, that was it. Let me tell you what happened."

The way it was—1854

Light Hair and his friend Slow were among the first to see the soldiers coming. The Long Knives were riding in wagons, sitting shoulder to shoulder. Behind the wagons a team of horses pulled a strange-looking object. It looked like a thick, short log, but it was black. A warrior who also saw the Long Knives shouted a warning.

Light Hair and Slow ran and hid in a chokecherry thicket. They knew the Long Knives were coming because of that skinny cow.

Several days earlier, a cow had wandered into the village. A cow from those whites called Mormons. The cow had knocked over meat racks and bumped into an old woman. A

Mniconju had killed it. He had been visiting in the Sicangu village. The cow had been butchered and the meat given away to old people.

Then the white man had come, and he wanted his cow back. He had gone to the one in charge of the Long Knives at Fort Laramie and complained. A messenger came from the Long Knives' fort to the Sicangu village's headman, Conquering Bear. The old man offered payment—several mules—for the cow. Foolishly, the Mormon wanted his cow, not the mules. One mule was worth more than that skinny cow.

Conquering Bear had done his best to avoid trouble. Next the Long Knife headman insisted that the man who had killed the cow be put in jail. Conquering Bear refused. So the Long Knives had now come to take the Mniconju.

The soldiers jumped down from the wagons and formed a line, pointing their rifles toward the village. Conquering Bear and two other men bravely walked toward them. The old man spoke with the soldier in charge. The soldier spoke loudly, angrily.

Meanwhile, Light Hair and Slow saw warriors gather-

ing in the village. Long Knives—the soldiers—were not to be trusted.

Conquering Bear offered more mules for the cow. The soldier leader's name was Lieutenant John Grattan, and he was angry. He demanded that the man who had killed the cow be brought to him. Conquering Bear again refused. When the old man saw there was no use talking, he and his two men turned and walked away.

The soldier leader shouted, and the soldier guns fired. The big black thing that looked like a log turned out to be a big gun. It was fired at the village. It boomed like thunder. Conquering Bear was one of the first to fall, severely wounded.

The waiting warriors attacked, charging the Long Knives. Light Hair and Slow watched, too young to join. Warrior guns cracked and boomed; the men swung clubs and thrust lances. The soldiers seemed helpless because the warrior attack was swift. Many soldiers fell, and some ran away. Those fleeing were chased and cut down, except for one. He was sent back to the Long Knives' fort. The soldier leader, Grattan, had been one of the first to fall.

Light Hair and Slow watched some of the warriors ride toward the Long Knives' fort. They heard later that the Long Knives would not come out to fight.

The badly wounded Conquering Bear was taken to his lodge. There Light Hair's father and other medicine men treated his wounds. But their efforts could not save the well-liked old man.

When Conquering Bear died, a man walked through the village shouting the terrible news. Light Hair was very sad when he heard. Without thinking, he found his horse, mounted, and galloped away across the prairie.

He was angry. He understood now why many Lakota did not trust the white people. They were loud and quick to anger, and eager to shoot their weapons at the Lakota.

Light Hair rode aimlessly, his thoughts full of the sounds and images he and Slow had witnessed. Sounds of the Long Knife rifles, and the big gun; images of the brief and furious battle, and of soldiers falling.

He found himself at the base of a hill. Tying his horse to a plum tree, he climbed the hill and took shelter in the shade. Later he took his horse to drink from a small creek nearby. Then he went back up the hill. He could not take his mind off the battle or off the old man who had died. When night came, he fell asleep.

Light Hair had no food. The next morning he awoke hungry, his stomach growling. So he drank water. Very slowly the day passed. He sat in the shade and walked around the hill. He took his horse to water again. Evening gave way to night once more, and he slept. Sometime in the night, the dream came.

It was a strange dream. A warrior on a horse rode across a lake. Mountains and storm clouds rose to the west. There was the sound of thunder, and a red-tailed hawk flew above the man and horse. As the horse galloped, it changed color, from black to blue to white and then red. Bullets and arrows flew at the man but did not hit him. Then the horse and rider reached the dry ground, and other men, who looked like the rider, rose out of the earth. They surrounded the horse and pulled the rider down.

Light Hair could almost feel their hands pulling. Then he awoke. His father and another man were shaking him.

"Wake up!" they said. "What are you doing here alone?"

"What happened then?" Jimmy asked, after his grandfather had paused for several long moments.

"They went home, back to the village," Grandpa Nyles said. "Light Hair's dad scolded him for wandering off without telling anyone."

"Who was the other man?"

"High Back Bone, but he was called Hump," his grandfather replied. "He was Light Hair's teacher. He taught him how to be a hunter and a warrior. The two of them were friends for life, until Hump was killed in a fight against some Shoshone. He was a strong man and a very good teacher."

"What about the dream?" Jimmy asked.

"We all dream when we sleep. Sometimes the dreams don't mean anything. But Light Hair's dream had a very strong meaning. He didn't tell his father until months later. Then his dad and another medicine man told him what it meant."

Jimmy was very curious. "What did it mean?"

Grandpa Nyles smiled and ruffled his grandson's hair. "That I will tell you later," he said.

4

The Bozeman Trail

INTERSTATE 25 CUT FROM SOUTH TO NORTH ACROSS Wyoming. From the city of Casper it traced the route of an old road.

"This interstate pretty much follows an ancient trail," Grandpa Nyles told Jimmy. "It was marked out by a white man named John Bozeman. So it was called the Bozeman Trail. He marked it out back in 1860 to show the way to gold fields in Montana. Soon other whites came along and used it. Problem was, it went right through Lakota territory."

"Our people didn't like that?" Jimmy ventured.

"No, they sure didn't. And there were even older trails here before Bozeman. One was called the Powder River Road. It was used by our people."

He lifted a finger and pointed without taking his hands from the steering wheel. "See those mountains over there to the left?" he said. "Those are called the Bighorn Mountains now. Our people called them the Shining Mountains."

It was hard not to notice those mountains. They filled the entire western skyline.

"Why?" Jimmy asked.

"Because the snow on the peaks shines in the sunlight," explained his grandfather.

They turned off Interstate 25 at a sign that said KAY-CEE, drove past a convenience store, and eventually turned onto a dirt road. Kaycee was a small town, even smaller than Cold River. They drove through it in less than five minutes. A few miles farther on they came to gullies and low spots.

Jimmy noticed that the grass was sparse here and the

land looked like a desert, no longer like the grass prairies to the east. His grandpa pulled to a stop, and they stepped out of the truck. Everything felt different as well. Perhaps it was the jagged mountains to the west.

"There was an army post here," his grandpa said, waving his arm in an arc. "It was called Fort Reno."

"Was Crazy Horse here, too?"

"He sure was. But there was another fort to the north. That's where the interesting things happened," said the old man.

"Then why did we stop here?" Jimmy asked.

"So you can see what he saw. Smell the sagebrush and feel the same sand under your feet."

They walked a ways into the desert. In the distance a small whirlwind swirled behind a rise, raising dust. Jimmy imagined it was a group of Lakota warriors on horseback galloping their horses.

After a few minutes they walked back to the pickup. Shortly after that they were back on Interstate 25, going north. Just over an hour later they saw a large brown-and-white sign: FORT PHIL KEARNY STATE HISTORIC SITE. They exited, then drove through an underpass and onto a narrow two-lane road. It took them to a turn-off to a gravel road.

As they approached the historic site, Jimmy saw a wall made of upright logs. It was not that high. Off to the right was the Interpretive Center, according to a sign.

"What happened here?" Jimmy asked. He already suspected that Crazy Horse had been here. Otherwise they would not be stopping.

"This is where young Crazy Horse became a war leader," Grandpa replied as he parked the truck. "He was only in his twenties, unusual for a war leader. It's one of the reasons Crazy Horse is considered so exceptional."

Inside the building were dioramas—three-dimensional displays of the fort's history. They showed soldiers and Lakota and Northern Cheyenne. A man in a tan uniform approached them.

"Welcome to Fort Phil Kearny," he said. "I can try to answer any questions you might have."

"Thank you," said Grandpa Nyles. "We're Lakota from the Rosebud Reservation in South Dakota. I'm taking my grandson on a tour of Crazy Horse sites."

"Ah, I see," the man replied. "Then you probably know more about Crazy Horse than I do. But let me know if I can help in any way."

A half hour later they drove away from the Interpretive Center. On the access highway they turned north and parked at the top of a hill. There the highway ended. Nearby was a tall, upright monument made of stones.

"That's about where the battle came to an end," said Grandpa Nyles.

"A battle? What battle?"

"We call it the Battle of the Hundred in the Hands. The whites call it the Fetterman Battle. Some even call it the Fetterman Massacre."

"Why?"

Grandpa Nyles pointed at the monument. "Come on. Let's look at that plaque."

ON THIS FIELD ON THE 21ST DAY OF

DECEMBER, 1866,

THREE COMMISSIONED OFFICERS AND

SEVENTY SIX PRIVATES

OF THE 18TH U.S. INFANTRY, AND

OF THE 2ND U.S. CAVALRY, AND

FOUR CIVILIANS,

UNDER THE COMMAND OF CAPTAIN BREVET–

LIEUTENANT COLONEL WILLIAM J. FETTERMAN

WERE KILLED BY AN OVERWHELMING FORCE OF SIOUX,

UNDER THE COMMAND OF RED CLOUD.

THERE WERE NO SURVIVORS.

"They got it wrong," Grandpa Nyles said. "There *were* survivors of this battle: hundreds of Lakota and Northern Cheyenne. And Red Cloud wasn't involved in it."

"But it says Red Cloud was the leader," Jimmy said, pointing to the plaque.

"Well, Crazy Horse was the biggest reason the Lakota and Cheyenne won the battle. December twenty-first, 1866, was the start of winter. The temperature that day was thirty degrees below zero."

"That's really cold, Grandpa."

"Yeah. When it's that cold, it's hard to take a deep breath. Imagine what it's like to ride a galloping horse."

The way it was—December 1866

Smoke rose into the frigid air from eighteen conical lodges, thin undulating columns rising upward. Footsteps crunched on the snow. One by one a few young Lakota men wearing elk-hide robes ducked into a lodge.

The lodge was on the west side of the village. The village was one of twenty-three along the Tongue River. This particular lodge was the home of a Lakota medicine man named Worm and his two wives, their daughter, and their two sons. One of the sons was Crazy Horse.

Worm had been called Crazy Horse. He was given the name by his father, the first Crazy Horse. So when he passed it on to his son Light Hair, he himself took the name Worm.

For the entire day and into the evening, dozens of young warriors came to talk with Crazy Horse. The elders, the old men leaders, had chosen him for a special task. This was part of a plan to defeat the Long Knives stationed in Fort Kearny on Buffalo Creek. Every warrior wanted to be chosen to help him with that task. But he would choose only a few.

For several years those Long Knives had been living in Lakota territory. That was against Lakota wishes. Furthermore, the Long Knives were there in violation of their own promises. They had built their fort even though they had promised they would not. All in all, the Long Knives were part of a bad problem for the Lakota.

That bad problem was because of gold. A long way to the northwest were the goldfields. Hundreds, if not thousands, of whites used the Bozeman Trail to get to the gold. They traveled by foot, on horseback, and in wagons. And the trail ran straight through Lakota territory.

Two other forts stood along the Bozeman Trail: Fort Reno, to the south, and Fort C. F. Smith, to the north. That made three in all, built to protect the gold seekers from the Lakota and Northern Cheyenne—to protect the invaders against those whose home it was. That made the Lakota and Cheyenne angry.

What was more, the Long Knives were reluctant to leave their forts. When they did, they did not stay out long. That made it difficult for the Lakota and Cheyenne to engage them in battle. Therefore, they could not fight them and send them away.

After many failed attempts to fight the Long Knives, a new plan was made. First, lure them out of the fort. Second, lure them into an ambush. Young Crazy Horse was given the second task. It was a dangerous assignment. If successful, it could mean the defeat of the Long Knives. And, once defeated, they might leave Lakota territory. So every young warrior wanted to be selected to help him.

Crazy Horse's part of the overall plan was simple. There was a ridge several miles from the fort. He and his warriors would act like a mother grouse leading a coyote away from her nest. She pretended to be injured. When the coyote came close, she flew away but landed close by. Each time the coyote approached, she flew away again. Doing this, she led the coyote far away from her chicks. Crazy Horse's task was to decoy the Long Knives. To lead them to the ridge—and to the ambush.

The chances of success were small, though the plan was good. For that reason, Crazy Horse had been selected to lead. *In order to ensure success, the warriors he selected had to be very skilled and very brave. By the time he went to sleep, he knew the warriors he wanted.*

A bitterly cold dawn revealed the landscape. There was already activity in the villages along the Tongue River. Hundreds of Lakota and Cheyenne warriors were on horses and riding north. It was the first day of winter and very, very cold. Every man was bundled in a thick buffalo-hide robe. Many had elk-hide coats beneath that. They also wore elk- or bear-hide mittens on their hands. Just as important, they carried weapons. After all, a battle could occur today.

No one really wanted a battle. But it was a necessary way to defeat the Long Knives. Every man was afraid. Most would not admit that to anyone but themselves. But part of being a warrior was facing their fears. That was called courage.

The cold was very intense. Mist billowed from the mouths of men and horses. Warm breath turned into vapor. It took a lot of courage just to be outside in such intense cold. Horses' hooves crunched sharply on the snow. On dry ground they were a loud clop, clop, clop, clop.

After they had ridden twenty miles, the plan for the day was put into action. Some five hundred warriors hid on either side of the high, narrow ridge—about half of them in the gullies on the east side and the others on the west. These warriors were the main body of fighters; they would wait in ambush.

Two smaller groups of warriors rode farther south. Nine were led by Crazy Horse. They were the decoy warriors: five were Lakota, two were Northern Cheyenne, and two were Arapaho. All were skilled riders and experienced fighters. Little Hawk, Crazy Horse's younger brother, was the only teenager in the group. As a small boy he had been called Whirlwind.

There was another small group of warriors that was also an important part of the plan. This band would attack the horse- and mule-drawn wagons that came out of the fort. Those wagons regularly drove west toward the forested slopes, where they loaded wood for the stoves in the fort. When the wood wagons had been attacked before, soldiers always came out of the fort to save them.

Grandpa Nyles gestured, indicating the north-south ridge. It was very narrow in one spot, with steep slopes going down on both sides.

"This is where the battle started and ended," he said. "On this ridge. But we have to imagine the land covered with snow, though not completely. And remember, it was very, very cold."

Crazy Horse took his warriors to a thick stand of leafless bushes. Hidden there, they waited. The other group—the wagon attackers—kept going and found another place to hide. Then everyone waited to see if the wagons would emerge from the fort. Everything depended on that.

Before noon the wagons did roll out of the fort, through a large double gate. They rumbled west on the road toward the forest. Two or three men rode in each, along with their axes and saws. They were going to gather wood.

The wagons followed the road. Soon they were even with the long, low ridge to the right. From a thicket of shrubs, the wagon attackers burst from hiding. Making their horses gallop over the frozen ground, they rode toward the wood wagons. Gunfire erupted from the warriors' rifles and pistols. More gunshots blasted as the men in the wagons shot back at the attacking warriors.

The gunshots cracked loudly across the ice-covered landscape. A battle between the attacking warriors and the wagon men ensued. After several minutes, the fort's west gate opened and soldiers hurried out. They moved in a column of twos, eighty in all. The first forty were mounted. The forty behind them were on foot. The column hurried toward the gunfire.

The Long Knives had carried out such tactics before. Each soldier had a rifle and a pistol in a holster. All wore heavy blue overcoats, thick leather gloves, and fur caps.

Crazy Horse and his warriors saw the soldiers emerge through the gate. An important step in the plan was happening. He held his men back, waiting for the soldiers to get farther away from the fort. If he attacked too soon, they might run back to the gates.

The commander of the Long Knives was in a hurry, so the soldiers on foot had to run to keep up. Before long, the mounted soldiers were far ahead. From his hiding place

Crazy Horse could see them. He waited until he could see most of the column.

In spite of the intense cold, Crazy Horse tossed off his buffalo robe so he could handle his weapons more easily. His warriors did the same. He turned to them as he took out his pistol.

"Follow me," he called out. "We do this for our people!" Without looking back, he urged his horse out of the thicket. In the open he coaxed it into a gallop. The nine other warriors were close behind him, all of them with rifles in hand.

Though it was warm, Jimmy shivered, imagining how cold it was for those warriors and soldiers.

"Was it really cold, like you said?"

"Sure was. Thirty degrees below zero, according to the thermometers in the fort. The decoys and Crazy Horse had been in that cold since leaving their villages before dawn. It had to be brutal for them."

"Does it ever get that cold at home?" Jimmy asked, trying to remember if he had ever been so cold.

"A few times," Grandpa Nyles replied. "Any temperature below zero is dangerous. You can get frostbite and lose fingers and toes. I saw a man who lost the tip of his nose. Worse yet, you can freeze to death."

"Man!" exclaimed Jimmy. "I hope that never happens to any of us. Did those warriors get frostbite?"

"I wouldn't be surprised. The stories don't say, specifically. But they were all outside in that cold for the entire day. I'm sure some of them suffered frostbite."

"So what did Crazy Horse and his men do, exactly?"

"Well, they distracted the soldiers, tricked them into turning and chasing them, the decoys. If that hadn't happened, I wouldn't be telling you this story."

Crazy Horse led his warriors into a meadow thinly covered with snow. The horses' hooves sounded like two dried sticks hitting together. The blasts of gunfire were loud, too, in the cold air.

The mounted Long Knives followed them, as Crazy Horse had hoped they would. Now came the most dangerous part of the plan. Crazy Horse and his decoy warriors had to act like the wounded grouse. They had to stay just ahead of the oncoming soldiers. To avoid being hit by a bullet, the warriors kept moving. They scattered over the meadow. Each warrior rode in a different direction, then turned and went in another direction. This made it very hard for the Long Knives to aim their guns. Moving targets are very difficult to hit. Amazingly, so far, none of the warriors had been wounded or killed. Now and then a warrior fired back.

Between the boom of the guns, Crazy Horse could hear the shouting of the Long Knives. Their leaders were in front, yelling at their men. Crazy Horse assumed the leaders wanted their men to move faster.

In the middle of the meadow, Crazy Horse did a very brave thing. He stopped his horse and dismounted. Then he lifted one of his horse's front feet, curling it back at the hock. Yanking his knife from its sheath, he scraped snow and ice from the bottom of the hoof. The snow and ice could make the horse slip and fall, taking its rider with it. When he finished scraping that foot, he picked up the other front foot.

Meanwhile, the Long Knives were still coming, and

gunfire still blasted the frigid mountain air. The lead Long Knives saw that one of the warriors had dismounted and was attending to his horse. That made a very easy target. Much of the gunfire was aimed at Crazy Horse.

Bullets whined through the air above Crazy Horse, like angry mosquitos. Those bullets were very high. The ones that hummed like yellow jackets were close, very close. Now and then, a bullet erupted in the snow and bounced off into the air. That kind of bullet made a very high-pitched whine, almost like a scream.

Crazy Horse finished with his horse's front hooves and next took up the back feet. The bullets were getting closer and closer. His tan-and-white mare did not flinch at the booming of rifles as her rider scraped the ice from her hooves.

"Wow!" exclaimed Jimmy. "He really did that?"

"He did," affirmed his grandfather. "But he was smart, an experienced warrior. He watched the soldiers. As long as they were firing from moving horses, he knew they couldn't aim very well. And the foot soldiers, who were still running, were too far back to be on the mark, especially since they were panting from the effort. So overall, the odds were in Crazy Horse's favor. Still, one of them could have gotten off a lucky shot. But, as we know, that didn't happen."

"Did the soldiers know it was Crazy Horse?"

"No. They hadn't heard of him. No one among the whites had . . . yet. All they could see were ten warriors, a small force against eighty well-armed, well-supplied soldiers. Their commander, Captain William Fetterman, was confident. He was sure his soldiers could defeat any number of warriors. By all accounts he hated Indians. He didn't think they were as good as soldiers."

"Oh. So then what happened?"

"Well, when the bullets were getting really, really close, Crazy Horse finally, calmly, mounted his horse and loped— not galloped—farther away. By then, the other nine decoy warriors were pretty much doing the same kinds of things."

"They were?" Jimmy's eyes were big.

"Oh, yeah," said Grandpa Nyles. "They were doing everything they could to make the soldiers angry. To make them keep chasing them. Remember, the place where the other five hundred or so Lakota and Northern Cheyenne fighters were waiting was four miles away. Also, all of this was happening when it was thirty degrees below zero."

"They did, didn't they, Grandpa? I mean, they took the soldiers to the ambush place, right?"

"Yeah, they did. Over four miles of frozen and uneven ground, covered with snow and ice. When they came near the ambush place, the warriors went down a steep slope. It was hard for the horses and men not to slip and fall. It wasn't easy for the foot soldiers, either. But they followed. They were angry—or too afraid not to follow their commander's orders.

"So on they came, following Crazy Horse and his warriors. They followed until they came to a long flat hill. It was called Lodge Trail Ridge."

The northern side of Lodge Trail Ridge sloped down to a wide gully. There it led to the Bozeman Trail, used by white gold seekers heading farther north. It was a familiar trail to the Long Knives.

From the bottom, Crazy Horse looked up and saw the

Long Knives. Several of them were at the edge of the crest, looking down. They finally seemed to be hesitating. Perhaps they had spotted some of the warriors waiting in ambush. Crazy Horse and his men fired their pistols at the soldiers. Return rifle fire splattered bullets in the snow near the warriors. After another moment, the soldier in the lead rode toward the decoys. Others immediately followed him. Soon there was a line of soldiers coming down.

Crazy Horse signaled his men to fire again. Then they rode onto the Bozeman Trail and turned north onto a very narrow ridge. It ran north to south. On either side were very steep slopes and deep gullies. In those gullies on the eastern and western sides, the warriors were hiding. They had been waiting in the frigid cold since dawn, their weapons ready. They were eager for something to happen. They were waiting for Crazy Horse's signal to spring the trap.

For the first time since early morning, Crazy Horse felt confident that the ambush would happen. Now, on the trail, he and his men acted confused. To the soldiers they appeared to be uncertain what to do. Meanwhile, the column of soldiers and horses poured down the slippery slope.

Crazy Horse let them get close, and then the decoys galloped away, as if trying to escape. The mother grouse was luring the coyote closer and closer.

Crazy Horse stayed back and sent his men on along the trail. He waited as the soldiers came closer. Suddenly he felt the intense cold as the wind blew across the ridge. He heard guns firing, and bullets hummed by. Still he waited. When he could see their faces clearly, he turned and urged his horse into a lope.

The last of the foot soldiers came off the ridge. Crazy Horse stopped again to watch them. He heard the thud of horses' hooves on the frozen ground. His heart thumped in his chest. The plan was succeeding.

He urged his horse on again. Catching up with his men, he raced northward with them. At the bottom of a slope, a creek curved across a low meadow. They rode for it, five men in one line, the other five in another line. They came to the frozen creek and crossed the ice carefully. Once on the other side the two lines of warriors separated. Then they rode toward each other, with one line crossing the other, like the fingers of two hands interlacing.

Two warrior scouts, one on each side of the ridge, saw Crazy Horse and his warriors. That was the signal! Rising up from hiding, the two scouts each fired two rifle shots.

All the soldiers were past the narrow ridge now, hurrying after the fleeing warriors.

From behind leafless shrubs and out of narrow old creek beds, the waiting warriors emerged. Many had been hiding and waiting under buffalo- and elk-hide robes. All of them had been holding their weapons beneath the robes, to keep them warm.

In a few heartbeats, the gullies were suddenly filled with warriors. Everyone was scrambling up the slopes. The warriors on the south side closest to Lodge Trail Ridge climbed upward. Their task was to get behind the soldiers.

As soon as the warriors could see the soldiers on the ridge above them, they started shooting. Once the Lakota and Cheyenne guns started firing, and their arrows started flying, they did not stop.

Crazy Horse and his decoys had carried out their plan. The soldiers were in the trap!

The old man looked at his grandson. Jimmy was completely enthralled by the story.

"Are you with me so far?" he asked.

"Yeah, Grandpa. The battle was starting, right?"

"Darn right! Our warriors scrambled up the slopes from both sides. The footing was treacherous, slippery. Their winter moccasins didn't have lug soles, you know. And it was cold, really cold! But that didn't matter to them."

Jimmy looked down the slope to the west and turned and looked down the slope to the east. He could see them, hundreds of Lakota and Cheyenne men. He could see the mist from their breaths as they panted. They scrambled up the slopes, some of them slipping and falling. All of them were carrying weapons.

"What kind of weapons did the warriors have?"

"Most of them had only bows and arrows. Some did have guns of some kind, a six-shot pistol or a rifle. But ammunition—lead balls and powder—was hard to get. So everyone had bows and arrows. It was said Crazy Horse had only four round balls for his rifle, so he used his pistol until he ran out of powder. Then he used his war club and bow."

Crazy Horse and his decoys turned their horses back to the north. They galloped across the meadow and up the slope. Already they could hear the continuous gunfire.

Crazy Horse saw warriors scrambling up the western slope. The eastern slope was obscured from his view. On the ridge all the soldiers had turned back south. They were scrambling as well, trying to hurry. The soldiers on foot were running. Those on horses were whipping their horses, trying to make them go faster. They were all trying to get back to the safety of the fort. Many of the soldiers were falling, hit by bullets and arrows.

As he rode closer to the fighting, Crazy Horse could hear the screams and shouts of the soldiers. Frightened horses were screaming, too. Then he saw something utterly amazing.

Many of the soldiers were running, crowding together on the narrowest part of the ridge, and warriors on both slopes were firing arrows at them. Crazy Horse saw a narrow dark line, the same shape as a rainbow. For a moment he was puzzled by it, but then he knew what he was seeing. It was arrows. Thousands of arrows coming up from both slopes! Thousands of arrows flying at the soldiers! For a time they formed a black arc. Inside the arc soldiers were falling, hit by the arrows.

Crazy Horse heard later that Lakota and Cheyenne fighters were hit by arrows as well. The arrows from the east slope arced and flew down the west ridge. Arrows from the west slope arced and flew down the east slope. Some of them hit warriors scrambling up the slopes.

Crazy Horse and his fellow decoys joined the battle. Little Hawk stayed with his older brother. By then the soldiers were boxed in. Their initial frantic retreat southward had been blocked. They had nowhere to go. So the Long Knives tried to find cover from the enemy guns and arrows. Some of them hid behind rocks large and small. Some hid in any depression in the ground. Others huddled together in small groups and fired at their attackers. But many had already fallen, struck down by bullets and arrows.

Crazy Horse and Little Hawk stayed to the west side of

the battle ridge. They joined a group of warriors firing at a few Long Knives behind a large rock. Those soldiers were firing rapidly and had wounded several warriors.

Crazy Horse talked with a Cheyenne warrior leader. They decided to flank the Long Knives behind the rock. One group of warriors, with Crazy Horse, would move left, or east. The other group, with the Cheyenne leader, would move right, or south.

At a nod from Crazy Horse, the warriors moved out, keeping low to the ground. Often they ducked behind bristly soap plants for cover. Crazy Horse spread out his men, instructing them to stay low and to aim carefully. They could not afford to waste their powder and bullets.

The flanking maneuver was successful, though some of the warriors were wounded. After a steady exchange of gunfire, only two Long Knives were firing back. At a signal from Crazy Horse, the flanking warriors charged the remaining soldiers. Crazy Horse struck one down with his war club.

That small victory was one of many that day. They were also battling the dangerous cold. Fingers and toes, not to mention noses and ears, were numb. Cold fingers dropped bullets and lead balls. They spilled powder. Still, the firing was steady, though from the Long Knives it was less and less.

Jimmy looked around from the narrow ridge on which they stood. He could imagine them, the warriors and the soldiers. He could hear the loud blasts of gunfire and even the shouting and screams of pain.

"How long did the fighting last?" he asked.

Grandpa Nyles was looking around, too. "Oh, less than an hour, I think. Maybe even only about half an hour from when Crazy Horse and his men gave the signal."

"Is that a long time for a battle?"

Jimmy saw a strange look come into his grandfather's eyes. His grandfather was a Vietnam War veteran, a U.S. Marine infantry sergeant.

"Sometimes ten seconds feels like ten hours," Grandpa Nyles replied softly. "So I think for both the warriors and the soldiers who fought here, the battle probably seemed to last forever."

"The words on that monument said there were no survivors. That means that all the soldiers were killed, right?"

Grandpa Nyles nodded. "Yeah, they were all killed. All eighty of them."

Jimmy stood silently for a while. "How did it end?"

"Oh, the last small groups of Long Knives were overrun by the warriors. It got down to hand-to-hand fighting. Scary and gruesome, at the end."

"How many warriors were killed?"

Grandpa Nyles shaded his eyes and continued to look around. "Well, there were a lot of warriors wounded. Nobody knows exactly how many. Some say around forty warriors were killed. One of those was Crazy Horse's best friend."

Jimmy looked up at his grandfather. "Who was that?"

"His name was Lone Bear. They'd been friends since boyhood. They were separated in the fighting. After it was over, Crazy Horse was looking around for him." He pointed down the eastern slope of the battle ridge. "He found him, down there somewhere. Lone Bear had been shot through the chest. But it was so cold, the blood froze around the wound and stopped the bleeding."

"For reals?"

"Yeah. He was still alive when Crazy Horse found him. He held his friend in his arms until he died. Everyone who saw that said Crazy Horse cried like a baby."

Jimmy noticed that his grandfather had brushed something out of his eyes.

"I would be sad, too," Jimmy said. "It's kind of sad just to think about it."

"Yeah, it is. Come on, let's start back for the truck."

Near the tall stone monument were some large rocks. They stopped, and from his trouser pocket Grandpa Nyles pulled out a bundle of gray sage wrapped in red cloth. He placed it gently on the largest rock.

"This is for the Lakota, Cheyenne, and Arapaho warriors," he said quietly. "We should never forget them and what happened here. But we have to remember the soldiers kindly, too. They fought hard. Their people shouldn't have been here, like they promised. If they had kept that promise, those eighty men probably wouldn't have died here."

From the rocks they walked to the truck in silence. Jimmy could still hear the gunshots, the shouting, and the screams in his imagination. Grandpa Nyles was very good at telling stories. When they arrived at the truck, Jimmy looked back toward the battle ridge.

"What happened to Crazy Horse after this?" he wondered aloud.

"Well, this was the battle that established him as a leader of warriors. Word spread quickly among the Lakota, the Cheyenne, and the Arapaho. He became a hero. But he was a reluctant hero. He didn't want to be a leader. He just wanted to be a good man and a good warrior."

"He *was* a good warrior, wasn't he?"

Grandpa Nyles unlocked the truck. "One of the best. But he was a good man, too. He was quiet and humble. He didn't brag. He didn't even speak loudly. That's what I like about him. There were a lot of good and brave warriors in those days. But not all of them were really good men. Not all of them were humble, like him."

5

The Tongue River Valley

JIMMY SAID VERY LITTLE AS THEY RETURNED TO INTER-
state 25 and headed north. He was still thinking about the
story of the Battle of the Hundred in the Hands.

"Why did they call it 'Hundred in the Hands'?" he asked
suddenly.

His grandfather smiled. "Before the battle happened, a
Cheyenne holy man predicted a victory in a battle against
one hundred men. He said the warriors were holding 'one

hundred in the hands.' That meant a victory. The interesting part is that there were eighty soldiers who came out of the fort that morning. The holy man's prediction was close."

Jimmy sat quietly until they reached the town of Sheridan. There Grandpa Nyles took an exit and then turned onto a narrow highway that went north out of the town.

"We're going to take a look at the Tongue River Valley," he explained. "Most of the Lakota, Cheyenne, and Arapaho people who were here had villages in that valley."

In less than fifteen minutes they came near to the river. On either side of it were broken hills. The grass was sparse but green, and there was sagebrush everywhere. Its gray leaves brightened the hillsides and meadows along the river. "This looks nice," Jimmy commented.

"Beautiful country," his grandfather agreed. "Crazy Horse liked it here—a lot. This was the western end of Lakota territory, which started at the Missouri River in the east. He wanted to live here for the rest of his life. His Oglala people were here when he was born, so he grew up around here."

"Maybe I'll live here someday," Jimmy declared.

After they had driven awhile, Jimmy spoke again. "Crazy Horse sure was in a lot of places. Way in Nebraska, Fort Laramie, and now here."

"For sure. But this is where he spent most of his childhood, in what is now central and north central Wyoming. It wasn't Wyoming then, of course."

"So what happened here?"

"A lot," answered Grandpa Nyles. "He lost his birth mother. He learned how to ride horses, use and make weapons, be a hunter and a warrior. Had his first girlfriend."

"Cool—well, except for the girlfriend part."

"Hey, don't knock it," his grandfather said, grinning and glancing at him. "It'll happen to you one day. But there was one thing he did that I thought was really 'cool.'"

"He learned to shoot bows and arrows?"

"Yes, but what I'm talking about is hunting. Starting as a young teenager, he was a really good hunter." He pulled the truck over to the shoulder of the road and stopped. "Lots of elk and deer around here. So it was fun to be a hunter. But the best thing he did was supply meat for the old people and the widows."

"Really?"

"Yeah, he sure did, and nobody told him to do that. He decided on his own to do it because his parents, and family, told him it was good to take care of the helpless ones. So he would kill an elk or a deer and bring it back for a family that didn't have a hunter—you know, the old people or a woman who had lost her husband and still had children to care for. He would just leave the meat at the lodge door of someone who needed it."

Jimmy was intrigued. He thought for a moment and then said, "I can do that."

"You can, and you will one day," Grandpa Nyles predicted. "Long as you understand that Crazy Horse didn't do it because he wanted people to notice. He didn't even want people to thank him. He just didn't want anyone to go hungry."

"Because he cared, right?"

Grandpa Nyles smiled. "Yeah, you got that right. Later in his life, after he got married, he and his wife would give away their food. He would give away his horses so that people could ride and haul their belongings."

"Wow!"

"Yeah, giving away a horse in those days was like giving away a car today. I don't know anyone who would give away a car. Do you?"

Jimmy shook his head. "No. I guess Crazy Horse was a generous person."

Grandpa Nyles smiled broadly. "I'm glad you know that word, and, yes, he was very generous. That's one of the things all Lakota people were taught to be—generous."

He put the truck in gear and drove back to the road. After a mile or so he turned onto a gravel road that mostly followed the river. There were many broad meadows on either side, good places that could hold a lot of lodges. They drove to an area with a sign that read PUBLIC FISHING. Getting out, they walked toward the river. A warm breeze swayed the grasses and the shrubs near the banks. Overhead, hawks soared on the air currents. Somewhere nearby a meadowlark and a redwing blackbird sang their bright, cheery songs.

Jimmy could understand why Crazy Horse loved this place. In his mind's eye he could see lodges in the meadow on the other side.

"Grandpa, did Crazy Horse marry his girlfriend?"

"No," his grandfather replied a bit sadly. "She was given away to someone else. That broke his heart. Her name was Black Buffalo Woman. Later, though, Crazy Horse married a woman named Black Shawl."

"'Given away'? What do you mean?"

"In those days, a girl's parents had a lot of control over who she married. Black Buffalo Woman's father listened to someone who didn't like Crazy Horse, so he gave her to another young man. But Black Shawl was a good woman. She and Crazy Horse were devoted to each other. They had a daughter."

Jimmy nodded quietly.

Grandpa Nyles said sadly, "But they lost that little girl. She got sick with a disease called cholera. She died from it, and she was only four years old."

"Sad things happened to him a lot, didn't they?"

"For sure," Grandpa Nyles said, sighing. "His birth mother died. One of his second mothers died later, and he lost his best friend, and then his daughter. Like you said, lots of sad things."

"Did he cry?"

"He sure did, especially when his little girl died. He stayed at her burial scaffold for days. He didn't eat, didn't drink water. He just cried and cried."

"I saw my dad cry once," Jimmy remembered. "When my uncle died."

"It's hard to lose anyone we love. Your dad lost his brother. They were very close. He cried because he was grieving. Just like Crazy Horse did."

Jimmy looked across the river. There were birds flying and landing in low willow shrubs. Nearby, insects were buzzing. "I guess even tough guys cry, huh, Grandpa?"

Grandpa Nyles nodded, glancing down at his grandson. "Yeah. When things like that happen, like to your dad and Crazy Horse, it's okay for tough guys to cry. Don't you ever forget that."

Jimmy nodded. "I won't, Grandpa."

"Good." His grandfather waved his arm. "So you can see why Crazy Horse liked this area," he said. "In 1877, when the United States government told him he had to live on a reservation, he said he wanted that reservation to be here."

"Was it, Grandpa?"

"No. I think the government promised him his own reservation just to talk him into surrendering."

Jimmy frowned. "That . . . that wasn't very nice."

"No, it wasn't. But I brought you here because this is where Crazy Horse spent the last year of his life."

"Oh, wow," Jimmy replied as a feeling of sadness went through him.

"Of course, he didn't know it would be the last year of his life," Grandpa Nyles quickly pointed out. "He was more concerned with the hard winter that year, and for the future."

"The future?"

"The Lakota and Northern Cheyenne had won a great battle against the Long Knives in June of 1876, at the Little Bighorn. Because of that, the United States government was angry and wanted badly to put Crazy Horse and his people on a reservation. Sitting Bull and his people, too. That winter of 1876 and '77 was very hard, in a lot of different ways."

Jimmy knew about the Battle of the Little Bighorn. Grandpa Nyles talked about it a lot. But he hadn't talked much about what happened after the battle.

"What do you mean?" he asked. "How was it hard?"

"Well, it was a cold winter, without much food," Grandpa Nyles explained. "The buffalo were all but gone. White hunters had come for many years and killed them. Killed them for their tongues and hides. For sport. Eventually they killed most of the buffalo, so it was hard to find enough food to feed everyone. Ammunition for the guns was scarce and hard to get. Long Knives attacked them and burned what little food they did have. On top of all that, most of the Lakota had already surrendered. Men like Red Cloud and Spotted Tail were telling Crazy Horse and his people they should surrender to the whites, too. If they didn't surrender, the Long Knives would kill or capture them all."

"Geez, Grandpa. That was bad."

"Crazy Horse did a lot of thinking, spent a lot of time alone," Grandpa Nyles went on. "He didn't want to surrender—no one did. But the scary thing was, if they didn't starve to death, the soldiers would eventually come. There were hundreds and hundreds of them, with plenty of guns and bullets. Crazy Horse had only a hundred and twenty-eight warriors."

"He did surrender, didn't he?"

"Yeah, he had to. He was worried most about the helpless ones—you know, the widows, the old people, the children." Grandpa Nyles put a hand on Jimmy's shoulder. "He and his warriors could die fighting the whites, but who would take care of the helpless ones after that? Who would protect them?

"Crazy Horse and his council of old men decided it was better to live under the control of the whites, and stick together, and get through it somehow." He gazed out across the land. "They decided to surrender, to leave this place."

"But—but they won that last battle. You said so," Jimmy protested.

"They did, they won the last two battles," Grandpa Nyles said, a serious look on his face. He pointed south. "Over those hills was a battle that happened before the Little Bighorn. Over there is Rosebud Creek. Crazy Horse led about five hundred men more than fifty miles, in the dark of night, no moon. That next dawn they faced General George Crook's army, which had three times more men and a heck of lot more guns and bullets."

"For reals?"

"Yeah. The Rosebud Battle, the whites called it. We know it as the Battle Where the Girl Saved Her Brother."

Jimmy was intrigued. "Why?"

"Because a young Cheyenne woman rode with the men. When her brother's horse was shot down, she raced in to rescue him. Soldiers were shooting at her from two sides, but she still managed to save him."

Jimmy's eyes were wide. "Wow! Awesome!"

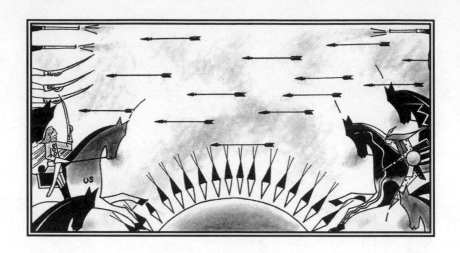

6

Little Bighorn Battlefield National Monument

JIMMY AND HIS GRANDFATHER CROSSED INTO THEIR third state in four days. First it was Nebraska, then Wyoming. Now Jimmy watched as they drove by the WELCOME TO MONTANA sign on Interstate 90 going north.

Less than an hour later they turned right at the exit to Little Bighorn Battlefield National Monument. Past a convenience store on the left and then a log trading post and restaurant farther up the hill, they turned right again.

A two-lane road led up to a tiny stone building just in front of the entrance and exit gates. Grandpa Nyles paid the fee and took a brochure from the young park ranger.

Jimmy looked around at the hilly landscape. He had the same strange feeling he'd had at the Hundred in the Hands battlefield. He felt like he should be quiet or talk only in a whisper. There was one thing that he could not figure out. The whites had lost the battle, and yet they wanted to remember it.

Past the gate they followed the road toward the parking lot. Off to the right were houses. At the western edge of the parking lot was a two-story stone building. The parking area went farther to the south, bending slightly to the east. South of the stone building was a cemetery with rows and rows of white headstones.

At the southern end of the parking lot were two more buildings. The first housed bathrooms, and the other, larger building was the visitor center.

Grandpa Nyles drove slowly through the parking lot, a slight frown on his face. "Tell you what," he said. "Let's do the battlefield first, then finish at the visitor center."

Jimmy nodded.

The parking lot was nearly full of sedans, SUVs, pickup trucks, and even a few motorcycles. Along the side of the road were large motor homes, some with cars in tow. Making a slight right turn, they drove up the hill. They got out of the truck and walked to the monuments. On the left was a new one dedicated to the Lakota, Cheyenne, and Arapaho warriors. It was a wide circular pit with two openings, one on the east and the other on the west. On the hilltop to the right was an older monument. It was large and four-sided, and it sat atop a mass grave. In the grave were the white soldiers who had died 138 years before.

Below the monument were white headstones inside a black iron fence. There were no graves, only markers, each indicating where a soldier had fallen. One of them bore the name of George A. Custer, the commanding officer of the U.S. Seventh Cavalry. The Seventh was the regiment defeated by the Lakota, Cheyenne, and Arapaho on June 25, 1876.

The hill that the monument was on was known as Last Stand Hill.

Grandpa Nyles cleared his throat. "Many still believe that Custer and his soldiers fought to the last man, until all of them were killed. It's true that all were killed, but there was no last stand."

"There wasn't?" asked Jimmy. "What happened?"

"Less than thirty soldiers reached this far. One of them was Captain Tom Custer. He was the younger brother of George Custer. The other two hundred had fallen along the way. They were all down along a mile-long ridge. You'll see the markers when we go that way."

The paved road passed between the monuments and turned south. Grandpa Nyles decided they would drive to the far end of the battle site. It was a place called Reno-Benteen Hill, four miles from Last Stand Hill.

The way it was—June 25–26, 1876

The encampment filled the river bottom for two miles along the meandering river. To the Lakota, the stream was the

Greasy Grass. It wound north to south and had many bends. The encampment was on the west side, among some very large and tall cottonwood trees.

This enormous village of one thousand lodges had moved to the Greasy Grass River only two days before. But the people had been together for two months by then. The first gathering was far to the east, and smaller. At first there were only a few hundred people, but, as the days went by, more and more people came. The village slowly grew to a few thousand. They were responding to Sitting Bull's message to gather and talk about the encroachment of the white people. A month ago Sitting Bull had conducted a Sun Dance, the most holy and powerful of Lakota ceremonies.

People from all seven Lakota bands were there. So was a small group of Nakota. The Cheyenne numbered several hundred; the Arapaho were fewer than that. Some people had even slipped away from the reservations to join the gathering. By the time they moved to the Greasy Grass, there were nearly ten thousand. Almost one thousand two hundred of them were warriors.

Never before had there been so many horses in one

place. Large grassy flats west of the village were filled with nearly fifteen thousand horses. Such a herd was very colorful on the green prairie. Most of the horses were bays (brown) or blacks, but there were buckskins (tan) and sorrels (reddish) as well; only a very few were white or gray. A herd that size could eat all the grass on a large prairie very quickly. That was one reason the encampment moved several times. The people moved to new areas where there was grass for the horses to eat.

Horses were very important. Every Lakota, Cheyenne, and Arapaho family had several. Horses for riding carried people. Other horses hauled lodgepoles and folded lodges when the people moved from one place to another. Still others were used as warhorses, meaning they carried warriors into battle. The fastest runners were trained to chase buffalo. Horses were one reason the Lakota became a strong nation and controlled a large territory.

Eight days after the Battle Where the Girl Saved Her Brother, people were still talking about it. That battle had occurred a long day's ride to the south, along Rosebud Creek. Crazy Horse and five hundred warriors had fought *a thousand Long Knives. With the Long Knives were three hundred Shoshone and Crow warriors.*

After that battle, those Long Knives had turned back south.

The Moon of Ripening Berries, or June, was a hot month. This day was already hot at noon when Crazy Horse walked north through the encampment. People were busy visiting, cooking, hauling water, and taking horses to the river to drink. Children ran and played. Young men and older boys were posted around the large horse herd to keep watch. All in all, it was an ordinary day.

The sun was in the middle of the sky when a Lakota man appeared on the hill across the river. He was shouting.

"Long Knives!" he yelled as loud as he could. "Long Knives are coming!"

Only a few people on the south end of the encampment heard him. Some, though they could hear him shouting, could not hear his words clearly.

Gunshots suddenly boomed from the south—many gunshots. The first warriors who heard reacted immediately. Running to their lodges, they grabbed weapons—guns and bows and arrows, war clubs, and lances—and ran toward the sound of the guns. Some got on horses and rode.

Everyone at the south end of the village could hear the guns now. So much gunfire was not good and usually meant danger. So much gunfire usually meant enemies. It was better to think that and do something than to wonder and be confused. Enemies attacking were nothing new to the Lakota, Cheyenne, and Arapaho people.

Mothers and grandmothers gathered up children to take them to safety. Old men helped them, or instructed the young men to grab weapons and meet the enemy.

People shouted warnings. "Long Knives are coming! Long Knives are coming!"

The frightening news swept through the camp, moving like a sudden gust of wind. More and more people heard the gunfire. It was not long before everyone in the encampment seemed to be running somewhere.

Warriors emerging from the south end of the village saw two lines of mounted Long Knives. They were charging toward the village. Suddenly they slowed, and one line turned west and the other turned east. They made one long line, then stopped and dismounted. Some of the soldiers grabbed the reins of horses and led them away, behind the line. The dismounted soldiers began firing toward the village.

Crazy Horse had sprinted back to his own lodge. He had to avoid the men, women, and children who were also running. Black Shawl had his weapons ready. Taking them, Crazy Horse hugged her for a moment, then jumped on his horse and rode toward the firing.

Nearly a hundred warriors were already among the trees and shrubbery and firing at the line of soldiers. Crazy Horse joined a big, tall man named Gall, a Hunkpapa Lakota war leader. They talked and decided to charge the west end of the soldier line. At that end were many of the Shoshone, Crow, and Arikara scouts.

Crazy Horse and Gall shouted to the mounted warriors close by. Gall led the charge and Crazy Horse followed, and forty or so mounted warriors were close behind them.

Firing from the soldiers and the warriors was constant. Every moment was filled with the sound of gunshots. The mounted charge was fast and furious. The pounding hoof-beats of galloping horses mixed with the gunfire.

Grandpa Nyles paused. He and Jimmy were near a marker overlooking the river, which was below them and to the west. Grandpa Nyles pointed at a large building in the distance. It resembled a western movie–style fort.

"See that?" he said.

Jimmy nodded.

"Major Marcus Reno's soldiers—he was the one in command here—and the army's Indian scouts were in an east-west line even with that building and us. It wasn't there in 1876, of course. There were about a hundred and twenty soldiers, and the scouts. They were firing north toward the village—the south end of it. Gall and Crazy Horse charged that end of the line."

"What happened then?" Jimmy asked eagerly.

"The Long Knives and their Indian scouts retreated. Mounted fighters always have an advantage over an enemy on foot. The warriors chased the soldiers this way, toward us. More and more warriors from the village joined the fight, as many as two hundred, maybe three hundred.

"Major Reno ordered a withdrawal, into the trees along

the river. As the soldiers fled, the Lakota, Cheyenne, and Arapaho fighters rode in among them. The soldiers did not fight back very well. Some were running; others managed to catch horses and ride. They seemed very confused. For darn sure they were very scared."

Grandpa Nyles pointed to groves of trees below them, along the west side of the river. "About there," he said, "the soldiers tried to take cover, in trees like that. But our men were relentless. They fired guns and bows and started fires. They forced the Long Knives out of the trees. They fled this way, across the river and up the slope. They suffered many casualties crossing the river. Same when they scrambled up the slope. Soldiers were falling, hit by bullets and arrows."

Grandpa Nyles turned and pointed east of where they stood. "They managed to get that far," he went on. "There, in a meadow, they took cover. They put up barricades with saddles, boxes, with anything they had, even the bodies of dead horses. They dug shallow pits in the ground."

Crazy Horse listened to the excited young Cheyenne war-rior. The two of them were with other warriors on the

west slope of a ridge. They could see the fallen soldiers on the slopes below them. The blue clothing was easy to see against the green grass.

Above them the sun was high, and the air was hot.

"The Long Knives are digging holes, piling saddles and boxes, anything they can," the young man reported. "Some are on the hills to the south, digging holes. I think they know we have them surrounded. Our men are all around. Some are trying to get in closer by crawling in the grass."

Black Moon, another Lakota war leader, looked at Crazy Horse. "Some of our men think we should overrun them, get them all."

"What do you think?" Crazy Horse asked him.

"The Long Knives still have lots of bullets," Black Moon said. "They keep firing at us. One way is to wait them out. They may be low on water and food."

Gall was climbing up the slope. Crazy Horse waited until he joined them.

"I think we should wait," Crazy Horse said. "The soldiers cannot go anywhere. We can wait and talk about what to do next."

It was easy to see that Gall was angry. He was a big, strong man. The angry scowl on his face made him look very scary.

He was about to speak when a high-pitched sound filled the air. All the men near Crazy Horse looked north. They saw a horse and rider racing toward them. The man on the horse seemed to be making the sound. They watched and waited.

The man on the horse stopped to talk to a group of warriors along the river. A warrior pointed up the hill, toward Crazy Horse's location. It was plain to see the man was in a hurry. He galloped his horse up the hill.

He was a young Lakota warrior Crazy Horse recognized. In his hand was an eagle-bone whistle. It had a high-pitched sound. The young man was agitated.

"Uncle!" he said to Crazy Horse. "Long Knives at the crossing! They tried to ride across the river into the village! They were stopped!"

"How many?" Gall asked, looking toward the north.

"I do not know," replied the young warrior. "Many of them, I think."

Crazy Horse looked at Gall and Black Moon. "We will leave a small number of warriors to keep the barricaded soldiers from leaving. All other warriors should ride fast to meet the new attack."

"So there was another attack?" Jimmy said.

"There was," Grandpa Nyles said. "The Battle of the Little Bighorn was not one battle. It was really three. The attack that the young warrior told Crazy Horse about was the second—Custer himself trying to cross the river into the north end of the village."

"He was stopped, right?"

"Sure was, by a group of old men and boys. They delayed those Long Knives long enough for the warriors sent by Gall and Crazy Horse to get to the crossing." Grandpa Nyles pointed to the truck in the parking lot. "What do you say we go and pick up the story from there?"

After a drive of a few miles, they came to a wide, flat gully. It was known as Medicine Tail Coulee. They pulled over near a historical marker with a picture on it. Grandpa Nyles pointed toward the river.

"The soldiers could see the village," he said. "They thought it would be easy. Custer thought that Major Reno and his men were coming from the other side. He didn't know that Reno had been chased across the river and up the hill. Custer didn't know that Reno couldn't help him.

"Those old men and boys stopped the Long Knives before they could cross. Not long after that, warriors came from the south. Custer had to turn and go that way"— Grandpa Nyles pointed up a slope going north. "He had no choice. Warriors came from behind him, and then on both sides of his column. North was the only way he could go. So let's go again and trace their path."

He put the truck in gear and drove back onto the paved road. In a few minutes they were at the top of the hill. After driving through a cattle gate, he stopped at another set of historical markers.

They stepped down from the truck. They were now on a ridge that led to Last Stand Hill, which was about a mile to the north.

"Somewhere here," Grandpa Nyles began, resuming the

story, "one company of the Long Knives stopped. One company stopped twice or two companies did the same thing. Anyway, they stopped, dismounted, and faced the oncoming mounted warriors. It was a good attempt, but it didn't work. Our warriors were coming, and they were angry. The gunfire they directed at the soldiers was too much. The soldiers got back on their horses and rode north. From this point on, Custer's soldiers, his five companies, began to suffer casualties. That is, soldiers were being hit by bullets and falling."

Grandpa Nyles pointed across the meadows to the north. "Remember those white markers? They start right over there. Each one shows where a soldier was found, where he fell."

Jimmy was silent for a moment. "There are a lot of markers," he said somberly.

"Yeah, there sure are," Grandpa Nyles agreed. "Custer had, oh, about two hundred and thirty men with him. He and only thirty or so made it to Last Stand Hill. So if you do subtraction, how many soldiers fell between here and Last Stand Hill?"

Jimmy said, "Two hundred."

"Yeah," Grandpa Nyles agreed. "That's about right. And if we do a division to figure out percentage—divide thirty by two hundred and thirty—the answer is about fifteen percent. So Custer had lost about eighty-five percent of his men by the time he got to Last Stand Hill. No military commander wants those kinds of losses."

Grandpa Nyles paused and shook his head. He removed his straw hat to wipe a bit a sweat off his forehead. "Of course, the sad fact is that Custer lost *all* his men, including himself. Every man in the five companies he led was killed in this second part of the battle. That's why there are so many white markers.

"That's the sad part about war and battles," he concluded. "Doesn't matter who you are, what side you're on. It's still sad, no matter what kind of uniform you wear or the color of your skin. It's still sad."

Jimmy looked across the meadow. He could imagine all those soldiers falling in the grass, falling to the ground. Somewhere inside, he wished he would never, ever see the real thing. After a moment he looked up at his grandfather.

"What did Crazy Horse do, in this part of the battle?" he asked softly.

"Well," replied the old man, putting his hat back on, "I'll tell you, but first let me tell you what Gall did."

Dust rose from the hooves of the galloping Long Knives' horses. They were struggling up the long slope. Gall and the warriors were closing the distance.

They had raced across the uneven western slopes above the river. Arriving at Medicine Tail Coulee, they saw the soldiers running away. Most of the Lakota and Cheyenne warriors in the encampment had been in battles before. Furthermore, they had been trained to be war fighters since they were children. Eight days before, many had been in the Battle Where the Girl Saved Her Brother. They knew what to do.

Some mounted warriors veered to the right, others to the left. A third group stayed behind the soldiers. If the soldiers stopped, they would be immediately surrounded. If they kept going up the hill and beyond, they would be cut down as they rode.

At the top of the ridge, a group of Long Knives stopped and dismounted. They formed a line to face the oncoming warriors. The soldiers fired, but it did not slow the warriors. They returned fire even as they galloped.

Most of the dismounted Long Knives fired again; then all of them remounted. They hurried to the north.

The onrushing warriors kept riding and firing from horseback.

Farther north along the ridge, some Long Knives dismounted again. This time only a few fired at the warriors before remounting. They hurried to catch up with the other soldiers, who were galloping north.

The galloping horses were raising a dust cloud that hung just above the ground.

Warriors were on either side of the Long Knives, and behind as well. Soldiers were being hit and falling from their horses.

Gall whipped his horse to run faster. He was on the slope below the soldiers. He shouted to the warriors near him. "Get ahead of them!" he yelled. "Get ahead of them, dismount, and shoot at them from the ground."

Eight warriors urged their horses faster. They raced recklessly over the uneven ground and outran the Long Knives' horses on the ridge. The warriors dismounted, formed a line, and knelt to get a steady aim. One by one they opened fire with their rifles at the fleeing soldiers.

All the while soldiers were falling, and falling. Many of their horses were galloping without riders.

"So that's what Gall did," Grandpa Nyles said, pausing for a moment. "He was one of the main war leaders, after Crazy Horse. The warriors with him below the ridge were all very good marksmen. They hit a lot of the soldiers. No one knows exactly how many, but a lot of them."

He pointed to the truck. "Come on," he said. "Let's go back to Last Stand Hill."

Jimmy hurried and climbed into the truck. "So where was Crazy Horse?" he asked.

Grandpa Nyles started the truck and drove north, following the paved road. "When Gall was here, Crazy Horse was on the other side of the river. He had gone through the village, gathered a lot of warriors, and ridden north. Somewhere beyond where the visitor center is now, he crossed the river and went east. He took his warriors up the hills, and there they encountered some soldiers who had gone ahead. They chased those soldiers back.

"So what Crazy Horse did was to block the soldiers from going beyond Last Stand Hill," the old man went on. "Gall's warriors and others, Crow King and Black Moon, were leading warriors, too. They were chasing the Long Knives from behind. There was no way the Long Knives were going to escape. By then, oh, maybe five or six hundred warriors were involved. It was all but over for Custer and his soldiers."

Grandpa Nyles pointed west toward the river. It was at the bottom of the slope behind the trees. "Right about here, some of the soldiers went toward the river," he said. "They made it to a deep gully and were surrounded there by warriors coming up from the village. Those soldiers didn't make it out. They say they are still there, buried in that deep gully."

Jimmy looked down the slope. He saw several white markers on the slope below them. He was beginning to understand how difficult it must have been for the soldiers.

They drove into the parking spot near the large stone monument. From there they could see back along the road they had driven. Jimmy could see a lot of white markers.

"Crazy Horse led a charge against a group of soldiers, right about here," Grandpa Nyles said, "probably a company. He saw they were organized and fighting strongly. He inspired other warriors to follow him, and they wiped out the company. At first he was the only one riding at the soldiers, far ahead of the other warriors."

"Wow! Wasn't he afraid?"

"He probably was," Grandpa Nyles said. "But remember his dream, when the rider was untouched by bullets and arrows? Crazy Horse was untouched at the Battle of the Hundred in the Hands, and he was unhurt here, too. Sometimes you have to do things no matter how scary it is, or how scared you are. For days, and weeks, months, and years after that, the warriors who were there talked about that— how Crazy Horse charged ahead of everyone else. Look, we're still talking about it now."

Jimmy nodded slowly. The tall stone marker was nearby,

and several white markers were on the slope. Below the tall monument were more headstones—those inside the black iron fence.

"So," he said quietly, "the battle was over, after that?"

Grandpa Nyles nodded. "Yeah. The last group of soldiers with Custer fired a few shots. The warriors had them surrounded and fired back. Maybe once or twice more there was light exchange of firing. Then it was over. They say it became very, very quiet."

"Then what happened?" Jimmy asked.

"People came up from the village, the women mostly," the old man said. "They were looking for their husbands, sons, and grandsons. They wanted to know that their loved ones were safe. Many of them were angry at the Long Knives. So that's when it started."

"What? What started, Grandpa?"

"Well," Grandpa Nyles replied, his voice low, "the first thing was probably someone taking something off a fallen soldier—you know, a gun, bullets, maybe boots. Then someone took a knife and cut a soldier's body. All that anger was hard to hold back. So they began stripping bodies, taking things, and then mutilating them."

"'Mutilating'?"

"Cutting arms and legs."

Jimmy didn't know what to think. "Why?"

"Like I said—the people were angry because the Long Knives probably would have hurt women and children— shot them, even. And Long Knives had done the same thing to Indians—like at a place called Sand Creek, in Colorado— mutilated people, I mean."

He paused for a moment and took a deep breath. "I personally think it's a bad thing no matter who does it. But that's the way it was then."

Jimmy felt a bit sick to his stomach.

He could imagine Lakota, Cheyenne, and Arapaho women and children crossing the river and walking onto the battlefield. He could understand why mothers and grand- mothers would be worried about their sons and grandsons. That's the way his mom and his grandmothers were.

"So, what happened after that, Grandpa?" he asked.

"Well, the second part of the battle ended here," Grandpa Nyles replied. "But remember those soldiers on the hill, back there above the river?"

Jimmy nodded.

"They were the first part of the battle, and they would be the third part. We'll talk about it in a bit, but right now let's go see that monument to our people. How's that?"

Jimmy and his grandfather followed the path to the monument to the Lakota, Cheyenne, and Arapaho people. It was unlike the tall stone marker for the soldiers. This monument was round and sunk into the ground.

They entered it from the east opening. It was like an open-air room. Jimmy liked it immediately, even before he looked closer at all the pictures and words on the walls. The first thing that caught his eye was the metal sculptures outlined against the sky. The north wall was lower, and on the stone ledge were three metal figures. Each looked exactly like a pen-and-ink outline sketch of a man on a horse.

Grandpa Nyles noticed Jimmy looking at the figures. They seemed to be moving from left to right. "Those represent the three tribes who fought here on our side: Lakota,

Cheyenne, and Arapaho," he explained. He indicated the third figure, the last one. That one had a hawk on his head and was reaching to take weapons from a woman on the ground.

"That's Crazy Horse," the old man explained. "Or at least someone's idea of him."

Jimmy pointed to the woman figure. "Who's that?" he asked.

"I'm sure that's his wife," Grandpa Nyles replied. "It was customary for Lakota wives and mothers to hand weapons to their husbands and sons. And they had a saying that gave them encouragement and reminded them of their duty as warriors."

"What was it?"

"The women would say, 'Have courage and be the first to charge the enemy, for it is better to lie a warrior naked in death than it is to turn away from the battle.'"

"What does it mean?"

"It means that courage was a warrior's best weapon, and that it was the highest honor to give your life for your people."

"Oh," Jimmy said, in a low voice. "That's kind of scary, I think."

Grandpa Nyles put his hand on the boy's shoulder and nodded. "Yeah, it is, but that's what being a warrior was all about: facing the scary things no matter how afraid you were. That's what courage is. And what's more, it doesn't happen only on the battlefield. You can have courage and face the tough things that happen to you anywhere."

"Oh."

"Come on," Grandpa Nyles said, pulling on Jimmy's arm and pointing to the polished walls around them. "Let's go look at those carvings and the inscriptions on the panels."

There were twelve thick granite panels on the walls inside the circular monument. All were nearly four feet high and just over seven feet wide. They had images and words connected to the Battle of the Little Bighorn.

The words were from the warriors who had fought here, from Lakota warriors and the Cheyenne. The words of Wooden Leg, a Cheyenne warrior, were simple: "We had killed soldiers who came to kill us."

"That about sums it up," Grandpa Nyles said quietly.

The panel devoted to Crazy Horse also had words on it. They were not about fighting or battles. "We did not ask you white men to come here. The Great Spirit gave us this country as a home. You had yours . . . We did not interfere with you. We do not want your civilization!"

Jimmy was a bit puzzled.

"I think that explains why he fought so hard, why he didn't want to surrender," Grandpa Nyles said. "He was fighting just as hard for those who had lived before as he was for those living at the time and those who would be born later."

"Like us?"

"Exactly."

Some of the other panels were about the enemies of the Lakota and Cheyenne: the Crow and Arikara scouts who were with the Long Knives that day.

"They fought bravely, too," asserted Grandpa Nyles.

They finished looking at the granite panels, lingering reverently at the panel devoted to Crazy Horse. They walked slowly out the west entrance and followed the stone-covered path. Crossing the road, they walked east of the visitor center and paused on the path leading to a long, sloping meadow.

Jimmy looked toward the meadow and then turned to look down the slope toward the river. "Why did the Long Knives attack our people?" he asked.

"Well," said Grandpa Nyles, "there were a lot of reasons. The big reason was they wanted our land. So they had to get us out of the way, put us on reservations. In 1876, two groups of Lakota were still not on reservations. One was Crazy Horse's band, and the other was Sitting Bull's. The other Lakota bands were at Fort Robinson, in Nebraska, including the Sicangu, Mniconju, and Oglala. Their leaders, like Spotted Tail, Touch the Clouds, and Red Cloud, had already surrendered to the whites."

"Why did they surrender?" Jimmy wanted to know.

Grandpa Nyles sighed deeply. "Oh, the main reason was because they were afraid of the power of the whites. The whites had more guns, more bullets. They had big cannons. Spotted Tail and Red Cloud had traveled east to Washington, D.C. They saw the big cities of the whites. But the one thing that scared them most of all was how many whites there were."

"What do you mean?"

"There weren't many of our people left by 1876," Grandpa Nyles explained, "compared to the sheer numbers of whites. There were probably twenty thousand Lakota. At the same time, there were twenty-five million white people."

Jimmy's eyes grew wide.

"So the Lakota leaders, like Spotted Tail, knew the odds were against us. It was like one cricket trying to fight off a thousand hungry ants."

Jimmy could actually see that, a thousand ants against one cricket. He knew about ants. He knew how strong they could be just because there were always thousands, even tens of thousands, in one colony.

"What about Crazy Horse and Sitting Bull?" he asked. "Did they know the odds?"

Grandpa Nyles nodded. "They did, but they also knew what surrendering would mean. It would mean giving up being free. It would mean giving up living the old way. It would mean Lakota people would be forced to accept the ways of the white man. So they believed it was better to resist them. That's why this battle happened, here along this river.

"The whites knew they were a symbol to other Lakota," Grandpa Nyles continued. "As long as Crazy Horse and Sitting Bull stayed free, they were dangerous. The whites were afraid they might inspire other Lakota to leave Fort Robinson and fight. Many of them did that. They left and joined Sitting Bull and Crazy Horse here."

Jimmy looked down the slope toward the trees. Beyond them was the river, which they could not see.

Grandpa Nyles saw that he was confused. "Hey, let me finish the story of this battle, and then we'll go inside and grab a cold drink."

Jimmy nodded.

The last engagement—soldiers on a hill

For the first time today, Crazy Horse felt tired. He lay on his belly and looked through his binoculars at the soldiers in the meadow. After the soldiers running toward the north had all been wiped out, he hurried back toward the soldiers who had been left surrounded. Through the glasses he saw the barricades that had been hurriedly built.

Another column of soldiers had ridden in to join those already on the hill. As far as anyone could tell, there were over a hundred soldiers behind the barricades. Now and then, one or more would moan or scream in pain. Those were the wounded.

"They've been digging holes, too," Black Moon told him. Black Moon was a battle leader. His face was dusty, his clothes soiled, and dried blood spotted his arms. "They tried to charge out," he went on, "but we beat them back. What do you think we should do?"

Crazy Horse lowered the binoculars and looked around. The air was hot, and he was sweating. Though hundreds of warriors lay hidden all around them, none could be seen.

"All we have to do is wait," Crazy Horse replied. "Let the sun and the heat get to them, make them do something stupid. We can rest and wait."

Black Moon nodded. That seemed like a wise approach.

He had seen much death today and was not ready to see more.

A young warrior scurried on hands and knees through the grass and found Crazy Horse. "Some of the old men want to know what is happening," he said. "They sent me to find you. They want to know what you plan to do."

"What's your name?" Crazy Horse asked the young man.

"My name is Good Weasel, Uncle," the warrior replied. "My mother is Grass Shawl—she's a Blue Sky. My father is No Horse, Mniconju Lakota."

"Ah, yes." Crazy Horse nodded. "I know your family. Tell the old men we have these soldiers surrounded. Most of our men came back from the second fight. I think the soldiers might try to break out, but we're ready."

Good Weasel nodded. "I will tell them that, Uncle," he said, and crawled away.

The afternoon passed slowly on the ridge above the Greasy Grass River. Unseen warriors on a high hill to the south fired a few long-range shots at the soldiers behind the barricades. A group of soldiers tried a mounted charge.

They were forced to retreat, unable to break past the fierce Lakota and Cheyenne firing.

Good Weasel returned as the sun was dipping toward the western horizon.

"The old men are talking," he reported to Crazy Horse. "Many of them say we should not risk any more of our men. They say the heat and lack of water and food will defeat the Long Knives here."

Crazy Horse nodded thoughtfully.

Black Moon's eyes flashed, and he tried to catch the war leader's attention. "Many of our men are ready to attack," he reminded Crazy Horse. "We are ready to die in defense of our people. I think it would take just one or two well-planned attacks to wipe out all those Long Knives."

Again Crazy Horse nodded.

Grandpa Nyles led Jimmy to the visitor center. In a room just off the small museum stood a topographic diorama. It was a miniature model of the Greasy Grass River, the hills to the east of the village site, and the flood plain where the village had stood.

He pointed to a high point west of and above the river. "Here is where the Lakota snipers were," he said. Then he indicated the location of the soldier barricades. "That's a few hundred yards. A long shot for those snipers. Soldiers behind the barricades say they fired back and hit the snipers on that hill. That's very far-fetched, in my opinion. My great-grandfather—your great-great-grandfather—who was there, said the snipers ran out of bullets. That's the reason they stopped firing."

"So what happened to those soldiers on the hill?" asked Jimmy impatiently.

"Well, they lived," Grandpa Nyles told him.

"They did?"

"Yeah, for two reasons. First, the warrior leaders couldn't decide exactly what to do, and Crazy Horse was being cautious. He didn't want any more warriors wounded or killed. Then, secondly, scouts came back from the north and reported more soldiers coming. More soldiers than they had already fought."

"Wow!" Jimmy exclaimed. "How many men did we have?"

"A lot less than the white historians say we did," Grandpa Nyles explained. "I'd be surprised if we had fifteen hundred. Probably more like twelve hundred."

"So then what happened?"

"Sitting Bull and the other old men decided that the people should take down their lodges and go south. Remember, most of the people there were women, children, and elders. So they wanted to keep them safe."

"So the village was taken down?"

"It sure was. The warriors on the hill, those surrounding the soldiers, really wanted to wipe the soldiers out," Grandpa Nyles said. "But they saw it was even more important to take care of their families. So Crazy Horse left warriors there, probably less than a hundred, to make sure the soldiers stayed behind the barricades. So all that those surrounded Long Knives could do was watch thousands of men, women, and children leave and go south. They were lucky. If the new soldiers had not been so close, their fate would have been different. The barricaded soldiers probably would have all been wiped out."

Jimmy stared at the diorama, imagining a long column

of people and horses. A column made up of Lakota, a few Dakota and Nakota, Cheyenne, and a few Arapaho. He wished he had been there.

"That was the end of the third engagement," Grandpa Nyles told him. "That was the afternoon of June twenty-sixth, 1876. That was how the Greasy Grass Fight ended, also known as the Battle of the Little Bighorn."

Somewhere in his mind Jimmy could hear people shouting and guns firing.

Grandpa Nyles touched his grandson on the shoulder. "Hey," he said, "there's a tipi out back. Let's go see it, maybe rest a bit before we head on."

As it happened, the tipi was a real one. That is, it was made from buffalo hide. It did not rattle in the soft breeze, like canvas lodges did. They sat inside it, leaning against the replica Lakota chairs, also called "backrests."

"Can we come back here next year?" Jimmy asked hopefully.

"My thoughts exactly," his grandfather responded. "Maybe we can make it a family trip. We can bring your parents and your grandma."

Jimmy nodded and smiled.

Looking through the door, they saw other people walking around and cars driving into and out of the parking lot.

"A lot of people come here, huh?" Jimmy asked.

"Yeah. I think I read somewhere about six hundred thousand a year," Grandpa Nyles told him.

"Wow! For reals? That's a lot of people."

"For sure. But you know what? I'll bet, except for a few Lakota, Cheyenne, Arapaho, Crow, and Arikara people who come here, no one has the connection to this place that you do."

"Because your great-grandpa was here?"

"Yeah, but also because the Indian people here were our ancestors. Because Sitting Bull was here, and Crazy Horse."

Jimmy stared out the door, deep in thought.

"You've walked a lot of places in the past few days," Grandpa Nyles reminded him. "Places where Crazy Horse and our ancestors also walked. We occupied the same space they did, saw the same kinds of plants, heard the same kinds of birds. The only thing separating us is time."

He waved his hand. "Crazy Horse led a charge through

here, maybe right where we're sitting," he pointed out. "A Cheyenne warrior later said it was the bravest thing he had ever seen. That charge took out an entire company of soldiers—probably a big reason Custer's five companies were defeated."

Jimmy nodded, again hearing shouts and gunfire in his mind.

"The Greasy Grass Fight happened a hundred and thirty-eight years ago," Grandpa Nyles said. "Crazy Horse and the warriors were not the only courageous ones that day. The mothers, the grandmothers, and the old people in the camp had to be brave, too. You know what the message is that they left for us?"

Jimmy shook his head.

"The message is 'Do not forget what happened here.'"

Jimmy nodded. "I won't forget," he promised resolutely.

In a strange way, Jimmy felt like he was leaving a part of himself behind when they drove out of the gates. He was determined to come back as often as he could.

They ate lunch at the trading post café across the road from the battlefield. It was full of tourists. Jimmy paid little attention to them. As he ate his buffalo burger, he relived the stories Grandpa Nyles had told.

"We have one more official tour stop to make," Grandpa Nyles said.

"Where?"

"Fort Robinson," his grandfather said.

7

Fort Robinson

AFTER A NIGHT IN A MOTEL IN CASPER, WYOMING, Jimmy and his grandfather drove east. They turned off Interstate 25 onto Highway 20. Sixty some miles later they were back in Nebraska.

Grandpa Nyles slowed down a few miles from Fort Robinson and turned onto a road. There was a scenic overlook. The view was of hills and ridges toward the east, and prairies all around. Below them to the east was the broad valley on either side of the White River. Grandpa Nyles stepped down from the truck with binoculars in hand and waved for Jimmy to follow him.

He looked briefly through the glasses, aiming them a bit to the northeast. After a moment he handed them to Jimmy.

"Look at those bare ridges," he said, pointing.

Jimmy took the glasses. He immediately saw the ridges.

"In May of 1877, after weeks of travel, they came that far," Grandpa Nyles said. "I imagine from there they could look down into the valley and see Fort Robinson. That moment, when they were looking down, was a critical time."

"What does that mean, Grandpa?" Jimmy asked, still looking through the binoculars.

"Well, the winter after the Greasy Grass Fight was very hard," his grandpa said. "No game, little food, and it was hard to find ammunition. The soldiers attacked them once. Lakota people from Fort Robinson were sent up to talk to Crazy Horse and his elders. They were urged to surrender.

"In the end, Crazy Horse and the elders thought the welfare of the women, the children, and the old people was more important. Besides, out of a thousand people, there were only about a hundred and thirty warriors. Sitting Bull and his people had crossed into Canada. So Crazy Horse and his band were alone against the whites. They decided to surrender. That's what brought them here."

Jimmy lowered the binoculars and looked around at the land. It was a warm late-spring day.

"Was it like this, Grandpa, when they came here?"

"Probably was, same time of the year. The reason we're here is that at Fort Robinson, Crazy Horse did what I think was the bravest thing he ever did in his life."

"He did? What was that?"

The way it was—May 1877

Several riders had stopped their horses at the edge of the bluff. From there the valley below was green and peaceful. They could see the river to the south and many hide lodges among the thickets near the stream. Some of the lodges were made of canvas. West of the lodges was the Long Knives' place called Fort Robinson. Crazy Horse stared at the buildings.

"Cousin," said a voice next to him, "it's not too late to turn back."

Crazy Horse glanced at his friend Little Big Man. "And what would we do?"

Little Big Man pointed north. Behind them was a line of people and horses. Everyone was resting in the afternoon sun. "I think it's a mistake to go down there," he said firmly. "So do many of our young men. We're willing to go on fighting."

"I know. So am I," said Crazy Horse. "That's what warriors do. But what happens if we all die? What will happen to our women and children and old ones? Who will be left to protect them?"

Little Big Man sighed. "Those are difficult questions to answer," he admitted.

"We know the answers," Crazy Horse retorted sadly. "That's why we're here. That's why we decided to join all our relatives down there."

Little Big Man had no answer. He glared at the distant white-man buildings. Soon his glare turned to sadness.

A young man rode up to join them. "Uncle," he said to

Crazy Horse, "some of the people want to fix food and eat before we go down there."

Crazy Horse nodded. "Yes," he said. "There's no hurry. The new, strange life among the whites will wait. It will be there."

All too soon the meals were eaten and the fires put out. There was a strange feeling of uncertainty. Down in the valley was the Long Knife stronghold. East and west of it were many, many lodges. Lakota people were down there, perhaps ten thousand or more. Many of them were relatives and friends. But waiting, also, was a new and unknown way of life under the control of whites. That unknown made Crazy Horse's people reluctant to finish their long and arduous journey. In these last moments on the bluff, they were free. What would be their situation tomorrow? Would they be free? That was the question that made them all uncertain and sad.

There was no use putting it off any longer.

Crazy Horse sat with Black Shawl, his wife. "Stay with my mother and father," he told her gently. "I don't know what will happen. Whatever happens, stay with them."

Black Shawl squeezed his hand. The sadness in her husband's eyes was unsettling to her. She squeezed his hand again and gently touched his face.

"I will," she said. "We will be all right."

With a heavy heart, Crazy Horse left his wife and mounted his horse. As usual, he took the lead. Many of the warriors rode behind him. In a way, it seemed as though this was the longest part of the journey—from the top of the bluff to the bottom of the slope. At the end of the slope, and across a wide meadow, was the stronghold of the Long Knives.

Ahead of them, Lakota people were gathering among the buildings. The news had gotten around quickly: Crazy Horse and his people were coming in.

Several of the younger warriors moved up behind Crazy Horse. "Uncle," one of them called out, "we could charge the Long Knives. We could surprise them."

"Yes," said another, excitedly. "We could defeat them."

"You may be right," Crazy Horse said to them over his shoulder. "But later on the Long Knives would attack our women and children. That is their way."

The warriors fell silent. But Crazy Horse shared their feelings. He could feel their anger over the situation.

He saw a Long Knife in a white hat standing alone. Near him stood a group of older Lakota men who wore dark scowls on their faces.

Suddenly one of the warriors behind Crazy Horse began singing a Strong Heart song. His voice was loud, strong, and defiant. In a moment another warrior began singing, then another, and yet another. Soon the voices were many and could be heard from a distance.

Crazy Horse knew he could not stop them from singing. He also knew his warriors were angry and ready to fight. Anything could set them off. If something happened and there was an exchange of gunfire, the women and children would be hit by bullets.

He could hear the warriors pushing up close behind him. Hoping they would not rush past him, he kept his horse to a slow walk. Again he noticed the Long Knife standing apart. Crazy Horse knew the man. "White Hat" Clark, he was called.

Crazy Horse turned his horse toward White Hat Clark.

He stopped when he could clearly see the man's face. As he had hoped, the warriors behind him stopped as well, though many of them were still singing loudly.

Crazy Horse dismounted and led his horse toward the Long Knife. A few paces from the man, he stopped. White Hat Clark seemed puzzled.

Slowly, Crazy Horse lifted his rifle, holding it level with the ground. He was careful not to point the muzzle toward the Long Knife. In a moment, the man in the white hat realized what Crazy Horse was doing.

The Lakota leader was giving up his rifle: a sign of surrender.

White Hat Clark walked forward and slowly took the rifle. Crazy Horse then led his horse forward and held out the rein to the white man. The Long Knife took the horse as well.

Behind them, the singing stopped. Without his horse and gun, Crazy Horse turned toward his men. He gazed at them evenly, no anger or apprehension in his eyes, only a quiet calmness.

Jimmy looked up at his grandfather. The old man's voice had faltered as he told the story.

"What happened then, Grandpa?" he asked.

"Crazy Horse's warriors gave up their weapons, too. He was their leader; he showed them the way. There's no doubt in my mind that that was the bravest thing he ever did.

"He agreed with what his men wanted to do. He wanted to keep on fighting. He knew that the Lakota warrior was a better war fighter than the Long Knife soldier. There was no lack of courage or skill. The problem was numbers. There just weren't enough Lakota warriors. Not enough men, not enough guns, not enough ammunition.

"Giving up his rifle and his horse went against every-thing that he was, everything that he stood for as a warrior. He did it for the helpless ones, the old people, the women, and the children."

They got back in the truck and drove the few miles to Fort Robinson State Park. Jimmy felt it was a sad place.

Grandpa Nyles pulled into the parking area near the log buildings. Jimmy saw the low stone monument where Crazy Horse had been wounded.

"Do you remember his dream?" Grandpa Nyles said, making no move to step out of the pickup. "The dream he had when he went out alone, near Fort Laramie?"

Jimmy nodded. "I do, Grandpa."

"Do you remember the part where those men come out of the ground and surround the rider? The men who look like the rider? The men who took him down?"

Jimmy nodded.

"Well, let me tell you what happened after Crazy Horse and his people had been here for four months," Grandpa Nyles said. "The whites were afraid of him. After all, he had fought the great General Crook to a standstill at Rosebud Creek, and he defeated Custer at the Greasy Grass. They were afraid he would lead an uprising against them.

"On the other hand, some of the Lakota leaders were jealous of him. They were afraid the Indian Bureau would make him chief over them. So basically someone decided to get him out of the way. I think the intent was to send him to Florida and put him in prison there."

"Florida?"

"Yeah, there were prisons there. Indians from various

tribes were sent there, notably Cheyenne and Apache. Anyway, Crazy Horse knew there was trouble coming, so he wanted to talk to General Crook, the man in charge. He took Black Shawl to safety, to the village of his cousin Touch the Clouds, east of here."

"Touch the Clouds?"

"Yes, he was a leader among the Mniconju Lakotas, and it's said he was nearly seven feet tall."

"Wow!" Jimmy exclaimed.

"Anyway, Crazy Horse took his wife there and was on his way back when the Indian police met him. The Indian police were Lakota who worked for the Long Knives. One of them was Little Big Man."

"Little Big Man?" Jimmy asked. "Wasn't he a friend of Crazy Horse's?"

"He still was," said Grandpa. "But now he was working for the Long Knives. There were other Lakota men who were working for the Long Knives, too."

Jimmy sort of knew the story, but he waited for his grandfather to finish it.

"They escorted him back here," Grandpa Nyles continued. "He thought he would be taken to the commander's office. There he would have a chance to clear up whatever confusion there was. But they steered him toward that building there." Grandpa Nyles pointed to the log building behind the monument. "It was a jail."

Grandpa Nyles paused and stared at the building, then sighed deeply.

"When Crazy Horse saw where they were taking him," he continued, "he naturally resisted. He tried to get away. The only weapon he had was a knife. By this time a large crowd had gathered, a few hundred people here, watching.

"When the Indian policemen saw the knife, they surrounded him. Little Big Man grabbed his arms from behind. Some say Crazy Horse managed to wound Little Big Man. But when all this commotion was happening, because people were yelling, a soldier came around the building. He saw a Lakota fighting with the Indian policemen, so he thrust his rifle, with a long bayonet on the end of the barrel, at Crazy Horse."

Grandpa Nyles paused again and took another deep breath.

"The wound was serious—a mortal wound, as they say. He fell there, at that spot. Later he was taken to the post infirmary—the hospital, I guess. He finally slipped away around midnight. His father and his cousin Touch the Clouds were with him."

From a bag on the dashboard, Grandpa Nyles pulled out a small bundle of sage. "Come on," he said.

They walked to the monument. Once again, Grandpa Nyles laid the sage on the monument. He sang a warrior's honoring song. He reached up and wiped away tears after he finished the song.

Somehow it seemed fitting that they reached Cold River at sundown. The day was ending, and so was their trip. Jimmy's mom bounded out of the house when they pulled into the driveway.

It felt good to be home, to see his mom again, to hear her voice, to feel her hands caressing his face.

"So," Anne said, "how are my travelers?"

"Tired," Jimmy said brightly. "And hungry."

Anne laughed. "The tired part you can take care of in a few hours. The hungry part we can do something about right now. I've got food on the stove, and Grandma is coming in to join us. Your dad will be home soon, too."

She looked up at her father. "Good to see you, Dad. Good trip?"

The old man beamed. "A very special journey, that's what it was. The visionary journey of Jimmy McClean and his grandpa."

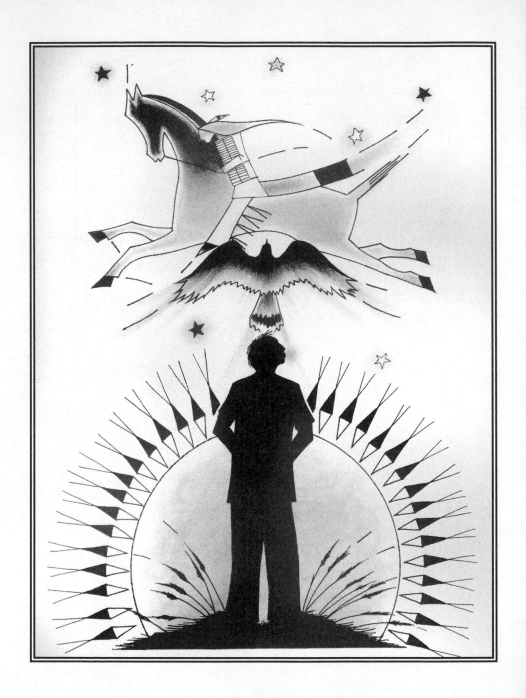

8
The Way It Was

SCHOOL STARTED IN LATE AUGUST. JIMMY WAS NOT looking forward to that, because he knew Jesse Little Horse and Corky Brin were still here. He was not surprised to see them standing together in front of the north entrance to the school building. A tiny shiver of fear went up his back. But he pushed it aside in his mind and walked toward the door.

"Hey," called out Corky. "Thought you might have left the country."

Jesse Little Horse simply grinned in that cocky, mocking way he had.

Jimmy walked past them without so much as a sideways glance until Corky reached out and grabbed him by the arm.

"Hey," he said, louder this time. "I'm talking to you."

"Yeah," chimed in Jesse. "Didn't think we'd have to teach you a lesson on the first day of school."

Jimmy could hear his grandpa talking in his head, that day on the Little Bighorn battlefield: *You can have courage and face the tough things that happen to you.*

He jerked his arm out of Corky's grasp. Then he turned and looked at his two enemies. "Come on, then," he said quietly. "Might as well pick up where we left off."

Jimmy stood, arms by his side, and waited. His calm gaze went back and forth between their faces.

Corky and Jesse were still grinning, but they noticed something about Jimmy McClean. He had grown a bit over the summer, so he was almost as tall as they were. But it was the look in his eyes that was different. They could tell he was not afraid.

Slowly their expressions changed. Their grins faded

away. Corky Brin glanced nervously at Jesse Little Horse. Jesse, Jimmy could tell, did not know what to do.

Jimmy, meanwhile, was still waiting. He was still calm and clearly not afraid.

He waited a bit longer. "Well, maybe next time," he said. Turning, he walked through the doors without looking back. He knew they were looking at him and he might have to actually fight them. But he was ready, and he knew they knew that.

Jimmy McClean had a feeling this year would be a better year. After all, Crazy Horse, when he was Light Hair, had endured worse than Corky Brin and Jesse Little Horse. If Light Hair could do it, Jimmy knew he could, too. No sweat.

Author's Note

IN MANY OF THE BOOKS I HAVE WRITTEN, I HAVE EITHER made Tasunke Witko, His Crazy Horse, the main topic or mentioned some aspect of his life, exploits, or character. Needless to say, he is my hero. Therefore, I am grateful to Howard Reeves at Abrams Books for this opportunity to write about my hero again, this time for a younger audience.

Growing up on the Rosebud Sioux Indian Reservation in South Dakota, with some time spent on the Pine Ridge

Reservation as well, I heard the name Tasunke Witko frequently. Some of what I heard was from descendants of Lakota people who lived in his time. By no means am I an authority on Crazy Horse—I am merely a student of his life and times, and I continue to learn more. However, as a Lakota, I do feel a connection to him because he was a real person, not an imagined hero.

One aspect of my life that connects me to Crazy Horse is bows and arrows. My maternal grandfather made primitive-style Lakota bows and arrows. Fortunately, he passed on to me the knowledge and information necessary to make them, but the skills to do so I had to develop on my own.

Each time I start the process and finish a bow and a set of arrows, and each time I shoot a primitive-style Lakota bow and arrows that I have crafted with my own hands, I cannot help but think of my hero. The simple and profound reality is that he made bows and arrows and used them.

For us Lakota who are aware of our history, stories are

a way to pass that history on, and to remember our heroes. Shooting a Lakota bow is another way that works for me.

I hope you enjoyed this story, but chances are you probably did not enjoy reading it as much as I enjoyed writing it.

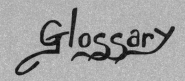

Glossary

ambush—a military tactic used in war in which combatants wait in hiding for the approach of their enemy

antelope—*see* pronghorn

Arapaho—a tribe of North American native people who predated Europeans and who lived in what is now northeastern Colorado and southeastern Wyoming

Arikara—a tribe of North American native people who predated Europeans and who lived along the northern part of the Missouri River in what is now North Dakota

arrow—a short wooden projectile tipped with sharpened stone or iron and sent from a wooden bow

Assiniboine—a tribe of North American native people who predated Europeans and who lived in the northern region of what is now Montana

bank—the soil edge where a stream or river flows, often eroded by the flowing water

barbed wire—a double strand of wire into which sharp barbs are twisted; used by ranchers and farmers to fence in domestic livestock such as cattle and horses

battle—a fight between two or more opposing forces made up of a number of fighters, usually with the use of weapons

Black Hills—the only mountains on the Great Plains, located in what is now western South Dakota and at one time within the territory controlled by the Lakota people

black powder percussion rifle—a firearm manufactured by Euro-Americans, capable of firing one round lead ball at a time, after which it had to be reloaded; the lead ball was propelled when a spark from a small percussion cap ignited the black powder in the back end, or breech, of the rifle barrel

bow—the part of the weapons system that sends the arrow; made by hand by the Lakota out of hardwood such as ash or oak

bowshot—the distance a Lakota bow could send an arrow, usually about a hundred yards

bullet—a projectile fired from a rifle or pistol

cavalry—soldiers or warriors riding into battle on horses and engaging the enemy as mounted combatants

Cheyenne—a tribe native to North America who lived on the northern Plains and were allies of the Lakota and Arapaho

cholera—a disease brought by Europeans and Euro-Americans to which native peoples of North America had no immunity; it was an infection of the small intestine that caused watery diarrhea and vomiting, and thousands of native people of many different tribes died from it

club—a hand weapon used by the Lakota and other northern Plains tribes, usually made with a wooden handle and a head of stone, iron, or the tips of buffalo horns

command—a military unit such as a squad, company, regiment, or battalion under the authority or command of one person

cooking fire—a small fire in a pit dug into the ground, over which food was cooked or water was boiled

cottonwood tree—a large hardwood tree common to the northern Plains that disperses its seeds on small white, cottony plumes that float through the air

coulee—a gully or ravine

coyote—a wild canine native to North America, larger than a fox but smaller than a wolf

creek bed—the bottom, often sandy, part of a creek or stream over which the water flows

Crow—a tribe native to North America who lived on the northern Plains; they were enemies of the Lakota, Cheyenne, and Arapaho

crow—a large bird found in North America, covered entirely in black feathers, with a raucous, annoying croak

Dakota—one-third of a nation of people living on the northern Great Plains, the other two being the Lakota and the Nakota; together the three were known as the Allied People

deer—an ungulate (which means an animal with hooves),

common to North America (and elsewhere), hunted
for its meat and hide by the native people of North
America and later by Europeans and Euro-Americans

diorama—a miniature replica of a building or part of a
landscape; dioramas are often used by museums to
depict historical events

drag poles—two long slender poles tied just above
the shoulders of a horse and extending behind it
and dragged by the horse; on the drag poles was a
lightweight wooden platform for carrying bundles or
people

fort—a military outpost; in this book refers to one
belonging to the U.S. government and sometimes
containing a civilian trading post located near or in
native (Indian) territory

Fort Laramie National Historic Site—located in
southeastern Wyoming on the site of the historic Fort
Laramie, operated and maintained by the U.S. National
Park Service

Fort Phil Kearny State Historic Site—located in north
central Wyoming on the site where Fort Phil Kearny

once stood in the early 1860s, operated and maintained by the state of Wyoming

Fort Robinson State Park—located in northwestern Nebraska on the site of the historic Fort Robinson, the place where Crazy Horse surrendered and was killed in 1877, operated and maintained by the state of Nebraska

four directions—west, north, east, and south, known also as the four winds or the four corners of the earth

frostbite—an injury to extremities such as fingers, toes, or noses caused by extreme cold temperatures; when frostbite occurs, the frozen flesh cannot be restored or healed

gelding—a male horse that is neutered and cannot sire offspring

Greasy Grass—the Lakota name for the Little Bighorn River

grouse—a game bird (one that is hunted) common to the Plains

gunfire—the shooting or firing of firearms, usually in a battle

gunpowder—the black powder made from sulfur, charcoal, and potassium nitrate used in firearms and ignited by a spark

hawk—a bird of prey (one that hunts) that inhabits the Great Plains; there are several species: a red-tail hawk was in Crazy Horse's dream when he was a boy called Light Hair

Hidatsa—a tribe native to North America who lived in permanent villages along the upper reaches of the Missouri River in what is now North Dakota and who now live on the Fort Berthold Reservation there

hoofbeats—the sound made when large hoofed animals such as elk, buffalo, or horses run, especially in groups or herds on hard or dry ground

Hunkpapa—the third largest of the seven groups of the Lakota; they lived in what is now north central South Dakota west of the Missouri River, and still do

Indian Bureau—the Bureau of Indian Affairs within the U.S. Department of the Interior

Indian scouts—warriors from native tribes who were recruited and employed to be scouts for the U.S. Army

kettle—a cooking pot made of iron; kettles were used by Euro-American immigrants and settlers and traded to the native people at trading posts

Lakota—one-third of the native nations of the northern Great Plains, which also included the Dakota and Nakota

lance—a long, very slender weapon for hunting and warfare made of a young pine or ash tree, about as long as the height of a man and tipped with a very sharp stone or iron point

Little Bighorn Battlefield National Monument—first known as the Custer Battlefield National Monument, the name was changed to Little Bighorn Battlefield in 1992; there are two different areas, with a visitor center located on the site of the 1876 battle, operated and maintained by the U.S. National Park Service

lodge—a tall, cone-shaped dwelling made of buffalo hides used by most of the native tribes of the Great Plains and elsewhere

lodgepole—a very long, slender spruce or pine pole used to support a hide lodge

Long Knives—what the Lakota called the soldiers of the U.S. Army because of the swords they carried

Mandan—a native tribe of North America who lived along the upper reaches of the Missouri River in what is now North Dakota, allied to the Arikara and Hidatsa and now living on the Fort Berthold Reservation

mare—an adult female horse

meadowlark—a small songbird with a bright and cheery call that nests in the grasses and low-growing shrubs of the northern Great Plains

meat rack—a set of long and thin horizontal stalks supported on vertical poles on which narrow strips of fresh game meat (from deer, elk, antelope, and buffalo) were hung to air-dry

medicine man—a healer among the Lakota (and other native tribes) who treated illnesses and injuries; many were also spiritual leaders and advisers

Mniconju—one of the seven bands of the Lakota

monument—a marker, usually made of stone, that memorializes a person or an important event, such as those at the site of Fetterman Battle of 1866 and the

military and Indian monuments at the Little
Bighorn Battlefield National Monument that honor
the participants of those battles

moon—the designation for "month" in the Lakota
language

Mormon—a group of white immigrants who, seeking a
home for their religious sect, traveled west along the
Oregon Trail in the mid-1800s and crossed through
Lakota territory

mule—the offspring of a male donkey (the sire) and a
female horse (the dam); the offspring of a female
donkey and a male horse is called a hinny

Nakota—one-third of the native nation that includes the
Lakota and Dakota, who lived on the northern Great
Plains and still do today

Oglala—one of the seven bands of the Lakota

Oregon Trail—the wagon road from Missouri to Oregon
and California used every summer for about twenty
years beginning in the late 1840s by Euro-American
immigrants looking for a better life in the west

peace talkers—the representatives sent by the U.S.

government in the mid-1800s to negotiate treaties with
the native peoples of the Great Plains

pistol—a handgun, usually a six-shot revolver, used by
both Euro-Americans and natives

powder—*see* gunpowder

pronghorn—a hoofed, horned animal, often called an
antelope or a goat antelope (although it is neither),
that lives on the Great Plains; the fastest land animal in
North America, capable of sprinting up to sixty miles
per hour

quarter horse—a breed of horse known for its ability
to sprint a quarter of a mile, now used extensively
on western ranches to herd cattle or to compete in
equestrian events

reenactors—individuals or groups today who portray or
otherwise act the part of historical groups or figures,
such as George Custer or Sitting Bull

reservation—an area of land set aside by the U.S.
government, or by a state (there are only a few), on
which native people agreed to live or were forced to
live

sacred—describing an object, a place, or an area considered holy or spiritually important, such as the Black Hills, which were and still are considered sacred by the Lakota, Dakota, and Nakota

sage—a grass and a shrub, each with several varieties, common to the northern Plains, used by many tribes as a smudge (smoke) in religious ceremonies

Sandhills—a region of low hills in northwestern Nebraska composed of sand rather than fertile soil

scout—a soldier or a warrior who moves ahead of the main body of soldiers or warriors to observe and gather information on the enemy

Shell River—the Lakota name for the stream flowing through Nebraska and Wyoming now known as the North Platte River

Shining Mountains—the Lakota name for the Bighorn Mountains

Shoshone—a nation of people native to North America whose territory was west of the Bighorn Mountains in what is now Wyoming

Sicangu—one of the seven bands of the Lakota

skillet bread—dough mixed with water and cooked in a skillet; an early staple of Euro-American settlers in the west and later of native people after they began living on reservations

Smoking Earth River—the name given by the Lakota to the river now known as the Little White River, which flows into the Missouri River in what is now central South Dakota

soap plant—a succulent plant with long, narrow, sharp bristles common to the northern Plains

Spotted Tail—a civilian and military leader of the Sicangu Lakota who was killed in 1881

stallion—the male horse, not neutered, and so capable of siring (fathering) offspring

Strong Heart song—a song of encouragement; Strong Heart songs were sung by both Lakota men and women to encourage bravery and devotion to duty, especially when an enemy was near and a battle was about to occur

tobacco—the inner bark of the red willow tree, which is peeled, dried, and shredded and smoked in a pipe;

later, native people used tobacco traded or purchased from Euro-American traders, today both red willow tobacco and commercial tobacco are used

treaty—a written agreement that resulted from the negotiations between representatives of the U.S. government and a native tribe and signed by both parties

treaty council—a gathering or meeting between representatives of the U.S. government and the leaders of various tribes and nations in the west, usually to negotiate a truce or the cessation of hostilities or the ceding of land to the United States

uncle—a title of respect to an older man when there were no blood ties (or biological relationship); as was also the case with "aunt," "grandmother," "grandfather," "grandson," and "granddaughter." This practice was due to the close ties of the extended family or *tiyospaye* and the importance of the entire village in raising and influencing children

U.S. Seventh Cavalry—the 650-man regiment under the command of Lieutenant Colonel George A. Custer that

attacked the Lakota and Cheyenne village on the Little
Bighorn River on June 25, 1876, and was defeated

wagon—the common mode of transportation used
by Euro-Americans in the west in the mid-1800s,
essentially a rectangular wooden box on wheels
with an axle at either end; some were covered with
canvas canopies and were called "covered wagons" or
"Conestoga wagons"

warrior—a war fighter; being a warrior was one of the two
roles or duties filled by every Lakota, Cheyenne, and
Arapaho male, the second being the role of the hunter

Whirlwind—a boyhood name likely given to Crazy
Horse's younger brother; he was given the name Little
Hawk as a young man

white—word used to describe a European or Euro-
American because of his or her pale complexion

white hunters—white men who came west in the mid-
and late 1800s to hunt buffalo only for the tongues and
hides; using powerful long-range rifles, they could (and
often did) kill hundreds of buffalo in a single day

white-tailed deer—a type of deer common to the Great

Plains, so called because of the white hair under their
long, wide tails

Worm—the name taken by the elder Crazy Horse when
he gave his name to his first-born son, Light Hair, who
became the Crazy Horse who is the subject of this book

woven wire—fencing material constructed in
crisscrossing horizontal and vertical lengths of wire

Bibliography

As always, my primary source is the Lakota oral tradition through the stories and cultural information told to me by many Lakota elders. I also consulted the following sources:

Andrist, Ralph K. *The Long Death: The Last Days of the Plains Indian*. New York: Macmillan, 1964.

Brown, Dee. *Bury My Heart at Wounded Knee: An Indian History of the American West*. New York: Bantam, 1970.

Buecker, Thomas R., and R. Eli Paul, eds. *The Crazy Horse Surrender Ledger*. Lincoln, Neb.: Nebraska Historical Society, 1994.

Hardorff, Richard G., *The Oglala Lakota Crazy Horse: A Preliminary Genealogical Study and an Annotated Listing of Primary Sources*. Mattituck, N.Y.: J. M. Carroll and Co., 1985.

Kadlecek, Edward, and Mable Kadlecek. *To Kill an Eagle: Indian Views on the Last Days of Crazy Horse.* Boulder, Colo.: Johnson Books, 1995.

Sandoz, Mari. *Crazy Horse: The Strange Man of the Oglalas.* University of Nebraska Press, 1992 (reprint of New York: Alfred A. Knopf 1942 edition).

Scott, Douglas D., Richard A. Fox, Jr., Melissa A. Conner, and Dick Harmon. *Archaeological Perspectives on the Battle of the Little Bighorn.* Norman, Okla.: University of Oklahoma Press, 2000.

JOSEPH MARSHALL III was born and raised on the Rosebud Sioux Indian Reservation and is an enrolled member of the Sicangu Lakota (Rosebud Sioux) tribe. Raised in a traditional Lakota household by his maternal grandparents, he learned the ancient tradition of oral storytelling. His first language is Lakota.

He is the author of nine books of nonfiction, three novels, a collection of short stories and essays, and several screenplays. As a speaker and lecturer, he has traveled throughout the United States and abroad.

Marshall has appeared in television documentaries and has served as technical adviser for movies. He was the narrator for the six-part mini-series *Into the West*, in which he also played the role of Loved by the Buffalo, a Lakota medicine man. He divides his time between South Dakota and New Mexico. Visit him at www.josephmarshall.com.

JIM YELLOWHAWK is an enrolled member of the Itazipco Band of the Cheyenne River Sioux Tribe and is also Onodoga/Iroquois on his mother's side. He is a multimedia artist whose work has been exhibited both in the United States and abroad. He resides in South Dakota. Visit him at www.jimyellowhawk.com.